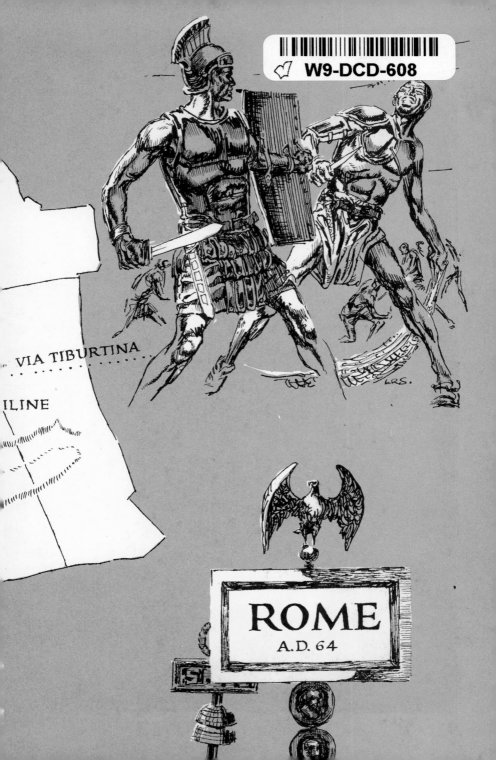

VIA TIBURTINA

ILINE

W9-DCD-608

ROME
A.D. 64

City of the Golden House

Books by Madeleine A. Polland

CITY OF THE GOLDEN HOUSE

CHUIRAQUIMBA AND THE BLACK ROBES

FINGAL'S QUEST

City
of the
Golden House

MADELEINE A. POLLAND

Illustrated by Leo Summers

A Clarion Book

DOUBLEDAY & COMPANY, INC., GARDEN CITY, NEW YORK

BURNS & OATES, LTD., LONDON

"For Fergus"

LIBRARY OF CONGRESS CATALOG CARD NUMBER 63–8751
COPYRIGHT © 1963 BY MADELEINE A. POLLAND
ALL RIGHTS RESERVED
PRINTED IN THE UNITED STATES OF AMERICA
FIRST EDITION

City of the Golden House

Chapter 1

The Roman legions marched victorious over two thirds of rebellious Britain and then they paused and took time to build a great road. Wide and straight, it slashed slantwise across the country like a sword cut, dividing Roman Britain from the still unconquered tribes who crouched behind their palisades and in their lake forts, watching for the day when the hobnailed boots of the legionaries would cross their road, and Rome would claim all Britain for her own.

"Though why, by all the gods, Rome wants it, I shall never know!"

On the sides of the new road, like a scar of frozen earth

across the dark fields, the piles of stones were edged with rime, and the grass was crisp and icy underfoot. The soldier who had spoken eased his frozen fingers sourly from the handle of his shovel and blew on them, his breath clouding around his face in the bitter air.

"Look at it!" His disgusted eyes roamed the dark hills beyond the road. Behind them the sun sank scarlet through the winter trees, and dusk had already fallen in the valleys. "It grows night again almost before the sun is risen." He wiped his cold red nose on the back of his hand and turned to look over the fields that sloped away behind him, covered in the distance with the vast sprawling camp of his Commander, and hazed with an icy fog.

"By Jupiter," he said, and shook his head. "What would my bones not give to feel a bit of sun."

He looked round for someone to grumble with, but his fellows worked on; it was warmer to keep shoveling than to stand still and complain. The only eye he could catch was that of a boy who had paused idly at a trough of cement, taking the iron bar to stir at it. The cold, complaining finger of the soldier was thrust out at him.

"You'll see!" the legionary said dourly. "You'll see when you get to Rome what a benighted, shivering heap of marshland your Britain is. You'll know it when you see a real blue sky and feel the heat on your back!"

The boy grew sharply still, his hands arrested on the iron bar. He was about thirteen, squarely and strongly built, his face ruddy in the cold above his brown frieze cloak, and his fair hair curling crisply to his shoulders.

"I?" he said, and his blue eyes were startled. "Why should I go to Rome?"

"Ha!" The soldier gave a sharp bark of laughter and turned to get his friends to share the joke. A couple of them grinned in something like pity at the boy, whose fair face creased in irritation.

8

"Why should he go to Rome, he says," the legionary went on. He thrust out his long neck sarcastically at the boy.

"Why should he go to Rome? Think you, young—what do you call yourself? Gretorix?—that the Commander in Chief stays here forever, building roads for barbarians? He has been fifteen years in this swamp, and now he goes home. Don't look so surprised!" He cackled with laughter, and now the other soldiers paused in their work and grinned openly. "We know. Don't you know the Legions know everything before Caesar himself? He is going home, and as you're his slave, you'll go too. Unless," he added happily, "he chops you first!"

The boy fumbled at the top of the cement vat, confusion and anger chasing each other across his face as he groped for an answer.

"I—I have a message for the Centurion from my lord Justus," he said in the end. "I must find him." He collected himself as he moved off. "And if he finds you lot," he yelled back at the soldiers, "leaning on your shovels like old women, you will have to buy your way out of a flogging!" He did not understand the curses that followed him. He had never sorted out these Roman gods. Grinning, he slowed down to think over what the soldier had said.

The Commander of the Roman troops in Britain, the Praetor Justus Gallius, had plucked him as a small child from the ruins of his father's burning village. Amused at the ferocity of the fair little Briton who had screeched and pummeled at the shining breastplate of his enemy, Justus Gallius had taken him into his own establishment, and here Gretorix had lived all his life, moving from one Roman encampment to another, body slave to my lord Justus since he grew old enough. He looked upon the Praetor as he would look upon a father, having known no other, and by now he did not know himself if he were Briton or Roman. In his simplicity, he had not thought but that this might go on forever. Now suddenly he knew that if Justus Gallius went to Rome, he would be a Briton no longer. He had had the best of both worlds: the shelter and the civilization of the conquering Romans, but in the land where he belonged.

He looked over the darkening countryside, chill and lifeless in the winter dusk, and his eyes were very different from the soldier's. He had been too young to fight the marching legions. He had taken them for granted. But to leave these darkening hills and the whole soft green sweep of England, never again to see the fields sloping to the shining river, or hear the cuckoos calling in the springtime from the dark woods beyond the hill. These things he had taken for granted and never thought about, until now he felt that he might have to leave them.

His steps grew slow with doubt and dismay. Perhaps that soldier was just talking for something to say. He shook his head. Around the fires of their camps and in their barrack blocks, the men of the legions seemed to pluck news from the air. If they said the Praetor was going back to Rome, then he probably was, even if he did not yet know it himself. Gretorix sighed and shook his head, and then ahead of him he caught the gleam of a scarlet cloak, warm and brilliant in the frosty dusk.

"Centurion!" he shouted, and suddenly cold, he began to run, his mind on his message, and his problem for the moment forgotten.

But it would not stay so. In the stout building in the heart of the camp that housed the Commander's headquarters, he waited on his master through the evening. The big room was sparsely furnished, but warm and comfortable in the red glow of torchlight, holding no hint of the bitter night outside and the cold that pressed against the shuttered windows. He looked at his lord Justus Gallius, and at his lean, familiar dark face with the graying hair cropped short around his head, his looks sharpened with the authority of Rome. All his life he had known this face and the even, steady temper of the man himself, as courteous and impartial to his humblest soldier as to his second-in-command, and ever warm with kindness to a homeless enemy who had no claim on him at all. Gretorix sighed. This man was all the father he knew, but if he were to be given the choice between him and Britain itself, which would he choose? One must be given up.

It was almost with relief that he heard the blare of trumpets two nights later, tearing the silence of the frosty dark outside the gates. He knew at once what it would be, even before the excited young Tribune on duty thrust aside the curtains of the door and announced the arrival of messengers direct from Rome.

They were hard on his heels, led by an old campaigning friend of Justus Gallius. They swept into the warm room in a swirl of plumes and scarlet cloaks, the metal of their breastplates dulled with frost, and carrying with them the hot, sweaty reek of their horses and the sudden, sharp breath of the night outside. Justus and his friend clasped each other's hands, their greetings warm with old memories and long affection.

"And what brings you here, Tertius? Not that I care. I am simply pleased to see you for yourself. But I doubt you have sailed all the way from Rome to wish Justus Gallius the time of day! Does Caesar wish me to press onward to the north before the road is done? It is not wise."

Tertius grinned amiably at his friend.

"By Jupiter, I swear you do not know why I come. You were always too modest, Justus. Have you not been long enough on the edges of the world?"

Slowly and formally, but with his amused eyes still on his friend's face, he unrolled the parchment and read out the command of Nero Caesar, that the Praetor Justus Gallius should at once return to Rome for duties as second-in-command of his Praetorian Guard. From the shadows, Gretorix watched his master's face, surprise and pleasure flickering across it in the red, uncertain torchlight. How can he be surprised, he thought, when every soldier in the Legion knew already? He shook his head. Young as he was, he realized there was a simplicity in Justus Gallius that expected no rewards, no matter how brilliant his successes. No wonder his friend smiled at him.

As soon as the Emperor's business was done, and the command accepted, Justus dismissed his staff.

"I would have my friend alone," he said, "to talk of old times and battles and rake the ashes of old campfires." His lined brown face was warm with pleasure as he looked at the other man. "Draw close, Tertius, my old companion, to the heat. Gretorix—you do not go. You will keep the goblets filled and see the brazier does not sink against these British winds of yours that search out every crack. My friend will not be used to them. Rome! Rome again, and the sun warm in my bones! I tell you, Tertius my friend, I did not think to see it again. I thought myself long forgotten, left forever to struggle here for more Roman fields to add to great Caesar's kingdom. For that is all he ever wins here, fields and swamps, and I had resigned myself to leave my bones beneath them. Who has now remembered me, to bring me back to Rome? Ah, good boy, Gretorix— the wine. Now draw your chair, Tertius, and tell me of Rome."

He leaned back in his leather seat, his goblet clasped between his hands and his legs stretched out to the glow of the brazier, his eyes expectant on his friend.

Tertius seemed unwilling to begin. His eyes were fixed on the glowing charcoal inside the copper bars, and for several moments he did not speak.

"Rome," he said at last, and raised his head to meet his friend's eyes. "You have been away a long time, Justus."

"Did I not say so? I last saw you in Gaul, and that was nearly twenty years ago! Before that—" His face grew closed, and his eyes dropped to the goblet in his hands. "Before that," he finished, shortly and reluctantly, "I was a tribune in the garrison of the Antonia in Jerusalem."

Tertius did not seem to notice his shadowed face or his change of tone.

"Then you have a lot to learn of the new Rome, my friend." He glanced around the shadows of the torchlit room, and raised his eyebrows at the boy who stood behind their chairs.

"He is my body slave. I trust him. What of Rome?"

"Rome is seething, Justus my friend. The young Nero has cast aside all those who may have guided him into sense and reason. He grows wilder as he grows older, and lives only to heap extravagance upon extravagance and folly upon folly. Some say he is mad. The people grumble as their taxes rise, and all they see for themselves are fresh fantastic capers from their Emperor and his chosen friends. Daily they cry out against him, and the streets are silent when he passes. Your new Commander, the Captain of the Praetorian Guard, is one of his boon companions. He owns the finest horses in the state, and can outrace Nero's own. That is enough to make him our Emperor's closest friend. Or enemy. Who knows? Least of all Nero Caesar himself. Close too, he holds the Senator Verius Bautus and his lovely, stupid wife, the lady Gallia—"

"The Captain of the Praetorian Guard, my new Commander." Justus interrupted. "That is Tigellenus, is it not?" Justus' dark eyes were sharp and considering. "What should I know of Tigellenus, Tertius my friend? Rumors have reached us even here in our forsaken land."

Tertius looked into his wine.

"Tigellenus? Know just enough to be very, very careful."

Justus reached a hand behind him to the table.

"This parchment says I am appointed Second-in-Command, but it seems to touch him that this is not sufficient to my rank, for he hints that I may get Command if he should move to a higher appointment. What higher appointment does he covet than being the Captain of the Emperor's personal bodyguard, the troops of the city of Rome itself? What appointment, Tertius?"

Tertius shook his head.

"I do not know, Justus. I do not know. But watch him. He would think no appointment too high for Tigellenus."

"Now tell me of someone more pleasing. What of my former victorious commander here in Britain, the good Aulus Plautius, and his lovely British lady, the dear Pomponia. We were children together. These are the friends I have missed most in all these years."

Again the round, amiable face of Tertius looked deeply troubled. He plucked at a loose thread in the wool of his tunic.

"She is well, Justus—well, and as beautiful as ever. But we fear for her. Justus, have you heard of the Christians?"

There was a moment of sharp silence before the other answered, and again his voice was short.

"I have," he said.

Tertius glanced at him. "Well, the lady Pomponia has become a Christian, these many years back I believe, but the secret was kept for some time."

"This I knew."

"They say now that only the fact that her husband Aulus Plautius is a hero, and a Senator, protects her. Her daughter too—you know her?"

"As a baby. Only as a baby."

"She too is a Christian, and her husband is the Prefect of Rome himself, Titus Sabinus. She is called Petronilla after the teacher Simon Peter, who, they say, baptized her as a child. It is *dangerous*, Justus, *dangerous*. Nero hates these Christians. There are thousands of them in the poorer parts of the city, and it seems they preach some nonsense of a Kingdom greater than the Kingdom of Rome. And Nero feels unsafe enough already. He fears the Christians, and I feel that someday he may grow vicious in his fear, and I tremble for your friends. When you reach Rome, Justus, try to talk to your dear Pomponia of this, and warn her of her danger."

"Tell me of this teacher, Simon Peter."

Tertius looked frightened as he sat.

"My friend, I do not want to know too much about them. If one values one's position, it is safer not to." He hitched his tunic over his knees and leaned forward into the warm red glow of the charcoal, the shadows etched deep into his anxious face. "They tell me," he whispered, "that some thirty years ago, there was a carpenter teaching all about this new kingdom, over in Galilee. They crucified him in Jerusalem. And now—" His voice was almost lost in his anxiety and fear. "And they say now, these Christians, that this man was the Son of God, the one true God. Imagine that. And this fisherman, Simon Peter, was his friend. He is an old man now. I beg you, Justus, as you value your friends, try to persuade them to forget all this nonsense— it is madness for people with positions in the State. It could cost them everything!"

Justus was not listening. His eyes were narrowed and distant, looking back into darkness in the past.

"Yes," he said at last to himself. "Yes. That I will never understand. This man Simon Peter was that carpenter's friend."

"Now, my good Tertius." His voice changed as he stood up and clapped his friend on the shoulder. "The orders you

15

bring say I must hand my command to you at once and leave for Rome. We have much to do." He looked at the sincere, troubled face of the other man. "I thank you, my friend, for all you've told me, and I will remember it." He shouted for the Tribune on duty and bade him take the Legate Tertius to his quarters.

He turned to the table at the side of the room as they went out, and poured himself another goblet of wine. His face was wry. "Well, Gretorix my boy, you have heard all that was said. We go back to Rome to an Emperor hated by his people. My new Commander is not to be trusted. All my dearest friends appear to be in danger of their lives. What a homecoming after almost thirty years of roaming the world! It may be that your swamps and fevers and my bones under a green field would be a better choice. Yet I suppose that we must go to Rome and take a chance on it."

His back was to the room and he did not see the agony of indecision on the boy's face. Were he a great, victorious commander, thought Gretorix, going back in glory to these Triumphs I have heard of, then I would make a bolt for it. I could get between the sentries on the road at night and join the tribes up north. I could learn again to live in a wattle hut and sew a wolfskin for my clothes. He grimaced and thumbed instinctively at the warm, thick wool of his tunic. But his master was not going home to glory. The days of the mighty victories were over long ago, and he had not been the one to go in triumph home to Rome. He had stayed through the long years to do a watchman's job, steadying the feet of Rome on British soil, edging the tribes toward the north for the last great sweep. And even that now must go to someone else. Gretorix drew a deep breath, and for the first time in days, his square, fair face relaxed.

"It seems to me, my lord Justus, we have no choice. We go to Rome and take a chance on it."

Chapter 2

In Rome the spring had come. Suddenly the sun was hot
and the shadows of the cypresses were sharp and black.
From the thronging streets in the center of the city the
warm distant hum of life crept up the hills, seeping through
the unshuttered windows of a room in a villa on the Esquiline; it mixed tauntingly with the perfume from the
blossoms on the sloping hillside and the sunlight that trembled in soft bright patches on the tessellated floor.

In the room a boy lay on a high carved couch, his head

turned wearily away from the slave who rubbed slowly and carefully at his legs.

"Enough, Fuscus." Suddenly he turned his head and his voice was sharp with irritation. "Leave it, I say. I am tired today, and it does no good. No good at all." On the last words his voice fell toneless, empty with resignation. Fuscus the slave stood up reluctantly, looking at him in doubt and concern, rubbing his large, supple hands on the front of his leather apron. There was silence in the high, cool room; a silence Fuscus could not break. An instant of fury and rebellion in the first days of his slavery had cost him his tongue, and now he could only stand mute and anxious, then bend hopefully again toward the boy. But the tired head turned away.

"No, Fuscus, no. No more today." He met the sad, dark eyes of the slave and closed his own. "Oh, don't look at me so with your dog's eyes! You have no need, my Fuscus, of your tongue. Your eyes say all you need. Do not despair, they say. Do not despair, my young lord Diomed—year after year I shall rub your legs for you, and then at last, suddenly, they will have the strength to walk again. That is what your eyes say, Fuscus, but it is no use. I have long despaired. No use at all."

The bright, silk-fringed pillows crumpled under his restless head; all that he could move since that spring evening just like this when the fever gripped him. Within a day his limbs were still. That was four long years ago, when he was eight, and Fuscus still stood there and rolled his eyes at him, pleading against despair with his dark, devoted face. Pleading while he stood on his own strong legs, with springtime restlessness in the air, and the clear shouts of running children from the distant streets. Diomed blinked rapidly at the painted birds that swooped across the pale plaster walls, and struggled to be calm. With an effort he spoke quietly to his dumb slave.

"I thank you, Fuscus, my devoted dog. You mean well. But I am tired. Send me Xania."

The huge Ethiopian clasped his hands and bowed, then padded on soft, dark feet to the chamber door. As though she had heard her name, Xania, the Greek nurse, brushed past him as she came in, knowing with one sharp glance at the boy that this was one of the bad hours, when shouting panic filled his helpless body and his brain rocked and split with his desperate need to stand and walk, just once, across the smooth, bright tiles toward the door. Despair was like a wolf at his throat, and all the patience of the long years vanished. The woman's eyes were quiet on his desperate face, and her hands quickly comforting about his pillows.

"It is warm, Xania," was all he said.

"It is warm, my young lord," she answered, and suddenly he was angered by the pity in her eyes. He was sick to death of pity.

"And the sun shines, Xania," he burst out. "And the flowers must be blooming in the peristyle. I can remember, you know! How I used to throw aside my sandals at the first sun, and run along the loggias to feel the hot tiles under my feet. Why can I not lie there now, even if I cannot walk! Lie and feel the sun on my face." His voice rose. "I can manage patience all the year but in the spring. Why should I not go out!"

Xania pulled at the heavy purple fringes of his quilt. This was a very bad day. He was usually so patient.

"Your lady mother," she began.

"My lady mother!" Diomed's voice was taut with anger, goaded by the bright day and a sudden wild rebellion such as he had never felt before. "Let us have truth, Xania! My lady mother is shamed by me. It is not proper for a beauty of Rome to have a cripple for a son! Oh yes, I know! She says I should be cool and quiet, in a room far from the bustle of so great a house. So I lie forever hidden in the shadows! For think—" His voice rose, shrill with bitterness. "Think who might not see me if I lay out in the sun. The great Nero Caesar himself, when he calls upon my mother unannounced in the afternoons to sit among her ladies in the garden, tinkling his lyre and loving his own voice, and shaking his curls and sucking sugared pomegranates!" He paused to look at Xania where she stood, her hands loose about an alabaster bowl, her scandalized face turning between him and the open door. "Oh, I hear it all," he went on before she could find voice to hush him. "The great Nero loves beauty. He could not be offended by the sight of me! Though if all I hear of his evil cruelty is true, he is even more crippled than I!"

At last Xania found her horrified voice, her hands to her own mouth as though she thus might silence him.

"My young lord," she breathed. "You must not speak so, or even your illness will not protect you. You lie here all day and listen to slaves' gossip, but you should know better than to repeat it." She plucked again at his purple spread, her hands trembling in fear and shock around the golden fringes. "And do not chide your lady mother," she added feebly, as if without belief. "She does for you what she thinks is right. And remember it is a great honor that Nero Caesar should so befriend the Senator your father, and the lady Gallia. Your father is one of his closest friends—this you know."

The young face on the scarlet, silken pillows was still hard and bitter, old far beyond its bare thirteen years with sickness and discontent.

"Yes," he said wearily, "this I know." He grew quiet and said no more, and the nurse considered his flushed, unhappy face.

"Demetrius the sculptor waits outside," she said doubtfully. "But I think I will tell him that today you are weary and should not be troubled."

Diomed's face softened and his eyes grew pleading.

"Ah, no, Xania. Let Demetrius come. He is good for me. He talks to me of the world outside my father's house and outside Rome, and even of the far parts of it beyond Italy. He tells me of all the countries where he has traveled. He tells me of Greece, his own country, and yours too, Xania. There the seas, he says, are dark as the stain of spilled wine, and the pale islands float on them like thistledown; and on the land, beneath the hot blue sky, the wind rattles through the olive trees that break up through the floors in the deserted cities."

He was lost now in the sculptor's words, never seeing, as he spoke of Greece, how Xania paused in her tidying of his room, how her hands grew still and her dark eyes wide with longing. He rushed on, unheeding.

"And he has been to Egypt, where the great lighthouse blazes over Alexandria, and the tombs of the dead Pharaohs rise like mountains above the yellow sands. He has told me of all this." Bitterness was forgotten, and the boy's thin, handsome face was suddenly young again.

"He has also been in Galilee," he began again, and then his talk faltered and his eyes clouded into puzzlement. Xania roused herself and looked at him, glad of his preoccupation, glad to see his mind turning away from himself. Through the high, square window the sun struck sudden gold from the carved foliage that crowned the pillars round his bed.

"Yes," she said encouragingly, "tell me what he said of Galilee."

"That is just the point," answered the boy, frowning. "For some reason, he will never talk of Galilee. All the other countries he will tell me of, but never this one. He has even been to Spain, to the western edges of the very world, yet when I ask him of Galilee, his face grows tight as if he suffers, and he will tell me nothing."

"It may be that something happened there which he is happier to forget."

"Maybe." The dark, brown eyes were reflective, and Diomed thought no longer of himself.

Xania looked competently round the freshly neatened room. Almost the only furniture was the large, beautiful bed, carved and gilded, inlaid with the pale gleam of ivory. It stood in a pillared recess, two steps up from the wide colored floor; beside it was the rich, soft blaze of a silken rug from the caravans of Persia, and a long table topped in fine mosaic. On the lower floor were a few chairs for those who came during the long days to bear company with Diomed.

The Greek sighed, satisfied with her inspection. A beautiful room, with the bright painted birds swooping on the plaster walls; but her lord was young, and the most lovely room a prison.

"Very well," she said, "Demetrius shall come." She turned to pick up the parchments that had slipped to the floor from the table beside the bed. "And who knows, my lord Diomed, but today may be the day he will relent and speak to you of Galilee."

The soft whisper of her departing sandals was followed by the struggle of two young slaves who staggered in with the heavy pediment on which Demetrius worked. Diomed watched them with eager eyes as they set it down.

"Now quickly, Pallius. Melas! Before Demetrius comes. You were let out last night. Did you go to the Circus? Who did you see driving? What horses? Any of my lord Tigellenus? They say they are the best now in the Empire; come quickly, tell me all of it."

The two boys were young Thracian twins little older than himself, who brought him secretly all the talk and doings of the young world outside which he might never join. They were all the friends he had. Now they turned, panting from their burden, their dark faces wide with grins. But there was a slither of sandals along the colonnade outside the door. Wiping the grins from their faces, they clasped their hands and bowed formally to their young master and to the Greek sculptor as he came in through the door.

He carried the clay head of the boy, wrapped in a wet cloth, and without speaking he set it on the pediment. Only when he had unwound the long folds of his toga did he walk up the two steps to stand beside the couch.

"And how," he asked then, "does my young lord Diomed today?"

He was a small, springy man of middle age and middle height, his gray hair a little long and wild about his head; quick and neat in all his movements, there was a steady watchfulness in his dark eyes.

The boy was truculent, cheated of his few moments of gossip with the slaves, balanced on the fragile edges of depression.

"And how do you think your lord Diomed does?" he answered rudely. "The sun shines beyond the windows and spring is come, but he remains among the shadows with the dead."

The Greek did not answer him. He moved slowly back across the sun-patched floor and took the wrappings from the clay head, moving round it with considering eyes.

"It was hot," he said then, "in the streets today. All the people in Rome seemed to have burst out of their houses at the first touch of the sun, and there was a rash of hustlers and hawkers all over the streets that would hardly let you move. A fellow has opened a new shop there at the top of Tuscan Street. He had a cargo of fine silks out of Cathay, spilling out into the street in all the colors of a peacock's tail. And the street before him was so jammed with ladies' chairs and litters that a mere man like myself must needs go round another way. So I walked down by Tiber."

Here he stopped as sharply as though a hand had been laid across his mouth, and his eyes grew wide and absent on the clay beneath his hands. Diomed stared at him, puzzled.

"Well then. You walked down by Tiber. What saw you there to silence you? Did the dead rise and walk, or what?"

For one moment the man turned to him and his eyes were startled, then he smiled a little, shaking his head.

"I was only going to say," he said easily, "that every urchin who could escape from school was there, dipping his pale, skinny little body in the river and chattering like an ape from Ethiopia. I watched them a little and then went to my home."

"And where do you live, Demetrius?" the boy asked idly.

"I live in an apartment house, beside the Vatican Hill and Nero's private gardens. I live on the fifth floor, the top floor, and have all Rome below me—even a seat for the chariot racing in the Circus if I am so minded."

The even voice flowed on, and the intent eyes slid backward and forward from the quiet, listening face to the clay under his hands.

"There," he said at last, stepping back. "How do you think your likeness grows?"

On the bright pillows, the tranquil face crumpled again into bitterness as the boy looked at the rough-shaped head.

"Oh, handsome, my good Demetrius! Handsome! What else should it be, so that my lady mother may set it up in her drawing room and bid all her guests admire her handsome son. No need to tell them that the rest of him is carrion!"

"Do not be so bitter, my young lord. Your mother has a

heavy burden in your sickness, and carries it as best she may."

Diomed laughed.

"Well, she has certainly gone to enough gods to try and get rid of it! I swear she has sacrificed to every god there is. With public dignity to Jupiter on the Capitol! Then coming slowly downward in her disappointments to the strange, dark, evil gods of the East, Mithras and Osiris, and their deathly rituals. She has even crept up the Vatican Hill at dawn in the month of the sacred pine tree, slipping through the oak groves with her offerings for the wild priests of Cybele, who slash their bodies with their own knives and are red with their own blood! How can that heal me?"

Now Demetrius stood looking at him as Xania had done, hands fallen to his sides, face drawn with dismay.

"You should not know of these things, my lord Diomed!"

"But I do know them, my good Demetrius! I do know them!"

Diomed was almost shouting, possessed of some wild rebellion born of the sun coming in his windows, longing today to shout and shock and have them know he was no helpless, thoughtless child who needed nothing but the comfort of his nurse. He was sick of Xania. Sick of her pity and her understanding, and his own dependence on them.

"When people come to visit me, Demetrius, they can only talk. And I hear much. They sit down there and talk, and soon forget that I am here. Others think that because my body cannot move, my ears cannot hear. No, Demetrius, I hear it all, and I know that what my lady mother needs is a new god, for all the old ones have failed her. She is still shamed by a crippled son. A new god, Demetrius, is what she needs. And so do I!"

He was so filled with his own wild restlessness that he

did not notice the sudden tense joining of the sculptor's hands or the sharpening of his dark eyes. In the long moment of silence that lay between them, Diomed caught a new sound and turned his eyes to the windows, breaking his thread of thought.

"Demetrius, what is that sound? It is like bees coming from a hive. I remember that from when I could walk. Or like a crowd talking as it walked through the streets."

The Greek turned back to his work, and his voice was guarded, as if he spoke to give himself time to think.

"Do you not imagine it, my young lord?"

"I do not. I hear it often when the wind is from the city. Be still and listen!"

Demetrius stood, his hand upon the pediment and his tunic sharply white in a patch of sun. Now his face was clear and careful; he seemed to have come to some conclusion and decided on something he must say.

"It is just what you think, my lord Diomed. It is a crowd that walks through the streets."

"Why?"

Demetrius looked at the bright, waiting eyes and picked his words with care.

"They follow a man called Simon Peter. A fisherman from Galilee."

The boy's face was wild with curiosity. Here was the forbidden topic.

"Tell, Demetrius, tell! Who is this Simon Peter, and why do people follow him? A Galilean fisherman in *Rome*? What can they follow him for?"

There was a long silence, as though the Greek hesitated before words that might never be called back. When he spoke it was as if to the colorless head on the pediment. He did not look at the boy.

"He preaches," he said, and his fingers were gentle on

the clay. "He preaches of a new God. Such as perhaps your lady mother seeks—and you yourself."

"A new god?" Diomed's voice was thin.

"Yes." The Greek glanced toward the curtained door, and his voice was still low and careful. "In all the talk that passes in your room, have you never heard of another Galilean called Jesus? A carpenter of Nazareth. Crucified—" The word fell with all the hesitancy of remembered anguish. "Crucified by Pontius Pilate in Jerusalem some thirty years ago." The man's face was stiff and dead, hiding what he felt.

"No." The boy looked at him with wide eyes, fixed by some sense of pain and urgency in what he said, some strange mystery that filled the bright corners of the painted room and drifted dark through the golden sunlight.

"He was the Christus."

"Ah," said the boy.

"You have heard?"

"Of the Christus a little. But when I asked Xania, she said the word must not be spoken in this house. My father, she said, is close friend to Nero Caesar, and so may only follow what pleases him. And for some reason this Christus does not. When I asked the younger slaves, they looked frightened and ran away. Then I forgot it. Who then is this man Simon Peter? What is he to the Christus? And *why* do the people follow him?"

"When Jesus of Nazareth preached Himself through the country of Galilee, there were twelve who went always with Him, and of these Simon Peter was the leader. And the first. Since the death of the Christus he has taken His teaching through all the countries of the eastern world, and men follow him to listen. That is what you hear—the people following him through the streets of Rome."

"You have heard him? Listened to him?"

"Often."

The boy was silent, staring at the sunlight on the pale colors of his walls, thinking rapidly over what he had heard. There was a hint here of Galilee, but not enough. He spoke again sharply.

"This Simon Peter—did you know him in Galilee? And was he then a follower of the Christus?"

Demetrius smiled, and his hands fell to his sides. He sat down in one of the ivory chairs with his elbows on his knees, and his eyes grew empty on the patterned floor between his feet. His spatula dangled idle in his long, fine fingers. He was remembering the Summer Palace of Herod Antipas, the Tetrarch, on the shore of the blue lake of Galilee, where he had worked on the frescoes through the chilly autumn days when Herod had departed for the lush vanities of his Roman winter. He remembered the huge, awkward young fisherman who had brought the baskets of his catch to the back door of the Palace; crusty and ill at ease under the teasing of the servant girls, he had thrown back his great curly head to laugh with scorn at the stories that the promised Messiah had already come, and was out in the hills above Cana, preaching of a new kingdom and healing the sick.

"Yes," said the Greek at last to the waiting boy, and his thin face was lit by a smile that was warm and gentle with affection. "I knew Simon the fisherman in Galilee—but he was not at that time a follower of the Christus."

He got up and turned back to his work.

Diomed was baffled. Here it all lay, he was sure. At the back of these small snatches about Simon Peter and the Christus lay the whole story of the Greek's unwillingness to speak of Galilee. Now he had begun, but the boy felt that his words but touched the edge of something—some excitement, some vast mystery that glowed in the sculptor's elderly face and brought crowds to follow a fisherman

28

through the streets of Rome. He did not know where to begin to question.

"But what, Demetrius—what does this man say or do, that people follow him? What does he tell of the Christus? What does he *do?*"

"He preaches, as I said, of the life and teachings of Jesus of Nazareth. Of the Kingdom of God that lies not in this world but in the soul of every man. And in the name of the Christus, whose love and whose Kingdom he preaches—" Demetrius turned now and looked full at the boy. He spoke as though his words were a gift he laid before him. "In the name of the Christus," he said slowly, "he heals the sick."

Diomed did not answer, staring back at him with eyes wide and dark as pitch, blazing with a confusion of hope and fear and disbelief. Into the silence came the flurry of excited voices and the scuff of hasty sandals beyond the door.

"Enough of this for today," cried Xania, bustling in with the young twins to take away the pediment. "There are far more exciting things afoot!" She noticed nothing of the fierce excitement already tense within the room, and Demetrius had to collect himself quickly to prevent his precious head from being dragged from under his hands by the two grinning boys.

"What *is* afoot?" he asked Xania as he laid it carefully on the floor and folded himself into his toga, not looking at the boy, who submitted in dazed silence to the freshening of his pillows.

"The lady Pomponia is here to call on the lady Gallia, and she has, she says, a special gift for the young lord Diomed."

The Greek did not answer, and his face grew still.

"There, my young lord," Xania chattered on, oblivious. "Now you are more fit to receive your guests. Tch! Tch!

What a messy business this sculpture is!" She stooped to gather up some fallen fragments of clay from the floor, and then, scolding and chattering, she shooed Demetrius through the door.

Outside, the pale, soft shadows of the spring evening were creeping along the pillared walks, and Demetrius shrank even more into the dimness of the archways to give passage to the brilliant group of ladies. Diomed's mother led them, hers the brightest of all the painted faces and the carefully tumbled hair, hers the brightest of all the embroidered tunics and floating cloaks that glowed and shimmered through the soft evening. Yet, even she was somehow dimmed by the woman who walked serenely at her side; older than any of the others, her fair hair streaked with gray, she was innocent of paint, and her tunic, cloak, and the scarf that floated from her smooth hair were all of plain unjeweled black.

Demetrius pressed himself against his pillar. The lady Gallia looked him up and down as if she questioned why he should be there at all. From under her black veil, the lady Pomponia threw him one glance of her fine eyes and did not look again.

Today the idle banter of his mother's ladies wearied Diomed beyond bearing. They crowded his cool, bare room with the swirl of silks and color and the heavy sweetness of their perfumes. He had no peace for talking to Pomponia, whom he loved, and their chatter beat like wings around his tired head. All he wished, most desperately, was to be alone and think in peace on this thing Demetrius had said.

"My lady mother," he said at last, and felt it more than he could bear. "Is there truly a gift for me?"

It was Pomponia who came up the two shallow steps to stand beside his couch.

"You are exhausted, my poor Diomed," she said. "I will

send for this present now, and then leave you with it. A dear friend of mine has just returned to Rome. He was in Britain, commanding the army of occupation. Now he is come back to the Praetorian Guard, and he has brought me a gift. I have decided to pass it on to you. You are too old now to be forever fussed with women, and you need company. You are too young yet to own this present for yourself, but I hold you responsible for everything to do with it. When you are seventeen, you can choose to own it for yourself or set it free." She smiled down at the boy's baffled face.

From Britain? Daily, a procession of readers and tutors sat beside his couch, and he groped in his mind for all they had told him of Britain. A far distant part of the Empire, somewhere on the edges of the world. To the north. Cold.

"A bear?" he asked tentatively, wondering what his mother would say to a shaggy monster in his beautiful painted room.

The lady Pomponia laughed. In a swirl of black draperies she went down to the door and clapped her hands, murmuring to the slave who answered her. The ladies were all silent now, as curious as the boy, their bright painted eyes fixed upon the door.

In silence it was occupied—by a boy of Diomed's own age, square and solidly built, his tender northern skin burned brick red by the southern suns of his voyage. His hair tumbled to his shoulders in thick heavy curls, as fair as Pomponia's own. He stood a moment taking in the pillared room, the swooping birds across the painted walls, the bright-eyed, silent ladies, and the unmoving boy upon the couch.

"His name is Gretorix," Pomponia said into the silence, and quietly the boy stepped forward until he stood at the foot of the steps below the couch and looked only at Diomed. He clasped his hands and bowed above them as

31

was proper in a slave, and then, against all rule and custom, he spoke before his master.

"So, my young lord," said Gretorix, and his Latin still held the roughness of his native fields. "I find we are the same, you and I. We are captives both."

Chapter 3

"Demetrius! What were you doing in the house of the Senator Verius Bautus?"

Pomponia's dark draperies lifted in the light speed of her walking as she crossed the atrium of her house. Along one wall the sculptor's chisel clicked and chipped on the gleaming marble of a fresco, and the white fragments piled below him on the colored floor. Behind her the fountains tinkled among the flowers into the wide copper bowl below the domed skylight, open to the blue springtime sky, and the pillared colonnades around the atrium were busy with the hiss and whisper of passing sandals and the murmured conversation of the slaves. When she reached Demetrius she spoke softly and urgently, that none might overhear.

"My lady Lucina," Demetrius began to answer.

"No, Demetrius, no. Not that either. You *must* be more cautious. Even in my own house I am Pomponia and nothing else. But why were you in the house of Verius? Is it wise?"

"My lady, I was asked to do a head of the crippled boy. It seems the lady Gallia was sent to me by the Emperor himself, for whom I have had the honor to do some work. Not that I have ever seen him, or he me. And I felt that to refuse the lady Gallia might only bring suspicion and notice."

"True, true. But be careful. I have known the lady Gallia long, and love her. She is foolish but not wicked. But her husband would go to any lengths to win favor from his Emperor. It is a house to be watchful in, lest we bring trouble on those who are not able to protect themselves as well as we are."

"You venture there yourself, my lady."

"I must. As I said, the lady Gallia and I have been friends since childhood. I cannot call attention by forsaking her. But once already, as you know, Demetrius, I have been brought before the courts on suspicion of following a forbidden religion. I do not *know* that Verius Bautus laid the charge, but I *think* so. And I say, Demetrius, be careful in that house."

Demetrius laid down his chisel. The vast atrium was quiet a moment, free of scurrying slaves, and there was no sound save the soft tinkle of water in the copper basins and the cooing of the white doves that flew in and out the open roof and strutted fan-tailed on the marble floor.

"The boy, my lady," he said. "The boy Diomed. I have

spoken to him. I felt such pity for him; he needs something to hope for, and when he asked me of Peter, I told him."

Pomponia's gentle face darkened with anxiety.

"What did you tell him?"

"Little yet. I told him of the Christus, and of Simon who follows him. And I told him that our master Peter heals the sick. I could not help but give him hope, my lady."

"It is done." Pomponia lifted her shoulders and smiled reassuringly at the anxious face of the sculptor. "I love Diomed as my own, so let us pray we have done well for him. You have given him hope, and I have given him a friend. You have more courage than I, Demetrius. I hope it brings the boy good and you no evil. I am protected, as you know, but you are alone, and there is no one to protect you." She laid a hand on his arm. "Have care, my friend, especially in the house of Verius." There was a sound of voices and a bustle of people coming through the rooms beyond the atrium.

Demetrius spoke urgently and quickly.

"Tonight," he whispered, "it will be at the house of Pudens on the Viminal."

"I will be there." Pomponia turned away from him to greet a man who strode into the atrium through the archway from the house, the sun through the skylight striking a blaze of silver from his Praetorian breastplate and the sword guard on his right arm. His plumed helmet was carried by a slave, and his purple cloak swept to the tops of his high leather boots.

"Ah, my dear Justus." Pomponia moved to greet him with a smile. "Your new uniform becomes you. How magnificent you look." She moved round him appreciatively. "You go to present yourself to the Emperor? We shall miss you when you move to your quarters in the Camp."

Justus Gallius bowed over her hand.

"To the Emperor and to my new commander, Tigellenus." He eased his shoulders under their weight of armor. "Magnificent, maybe," he said, "but I feel the weight of it. I was never tempted to cast away my cloak in Britain! Oh, Pomponia, it is good to be in Rome again after all these long, cold years."

Pomponia glanced at the water clock beside the pool.

"Are you not a little early? It is barely the fourth hour. Will Nero Caesar be ready to receive?"

"I am going first, as I promised you, in all my armor, to call on your young friend to whom you gave my Gretorix."

"Ah, you are kind, Justus, kind. A Commander of the Guard in all his glory will be a great pleasure to the poor boy. Give him Pomponia's love and tell him to care well for our present."

Diomed was caring very well for their present. Since the day when Gretorix had come, the marble colonnades of the house of Verius were in an uproar. The slaves attached to Diomed giggled behind their hands, and Xania wept and moaned in her quarters, refusing to be comforted.

Diomed was immovable.

"It is as the lady Pomponia said," he cried. "I grow too old to be fussed always by women. Let Xania care for my sickness if she must; let her tell Fuscus when he should rub my legs and arms, and feed me her foul potions that do no good. But now, for all other things, and for my company, I shall have none but Gretorix. He is mine, the lady Pomponia said, and mine alone. He shall tend me by day and sleep with me by night. Pomponia is right. I am sick of women."

An irritated Gallia gave way to him. Pomponia was important and should be pleased. Besides, she herself could do with another handmaid and would be glad to take Xania. Let the boy manage with his barbarian slave and give them all some peace. By the time the train of slaves who rode with the Praetor stood before the great outer door, order was restored. The grieving Xania was comforted with new responsibility, and the triumphant Diomed grinned across the room at Gretorix, whose sunburned face had stayed impassive through the uproar.

Diomed did not understand himself. Only the other day, he had almost screamed for the comfort of Xania's presence; he had for all the long years depended on her strength. Suddenly, in the moment when the fair-haired Briton had stood below his bed, he had known that whether he could walk or not, this boy would never pity him. "We are captives both." And from this there would be a new strength. Or perhaps the new strength had begun a little earlier, with the sudden, fearful statement of Demetrius, raising hope where hope was long since dead.

He did not know. He knew only that he greeted these muddled and ill-tempered days with excitement he had not known for years, and he cried out in pleasure when the Praetor Justus stood below his bed in all the glitter of his gold and silver and tumbling purple plumes.

"You do me much honor, sir," he said, "so to visit me."

Justus greeted him, and bade him give his regrets to his mother that he was too early to be received by her. He turned to the young Briton, who bowed formally over his clasped hands, but with pleasure and affection warm on his face.

"Well, Gretorix. And how do you continue to find our mother, Rome?"

The fair boy smiled slightly, and Diomed's sharp eyes flashed from him to the man, sensing the confidence and familiarity between them.

"Hot, my lord," was all he said.

"I'll warrant you do. So do I. Bring me some wine to cool me."

He watched the boy go out of the room.

"You must be good to him, my son," he said then to the young Roman. "As they know nobility in that barbaric land, he is of noble birth. I have had him since he was a small child and I took his father's fort. He is a good boy, Diomed. Care for him as I have done. He is yours now."

"Why did you give him to me?"

The man smiled.

"The lady Pomponia persuaded me," he said, "that your need of him was more than mine. She took a great fancy to this lad, and was heart-set that you should have him about you. Besides, I could not keep him in the Praetorian Camp."

"My lord Justus." Diomed acknowledged all he said about the boy, but his mind these last days was fixed on one thing. "My lord, how long are you back in Rome?"

"About ten days, my boy. Why?"

"Have you been out much in the streets of the city?"

The man looked faintly puzzled.

"Why, yes," he answered patiently, "I am delighted to be home." The strengthening sun struck through the windows to catch the white in the hair above his ears, softening it to the same silver as his gleaming armor.

"Have you seen or heard anything of a man called Simon Peter?"

Justus grew very still, and a look of caution crept across his soldier's face.

"What do you know of Simon Peter?"

"Very little, but I would know much more." Gretorix came back with the wine, and Diomed waited patiently while he served it and Justus took his first long draught.

"Have you seen him, my lord?" he pressed, as the man set his goblet down.

"I have seen him." The Praetor seemed reluctant to

speak. He went on almost as though he were compelled to talk of it. "I have seen him. And I do not understand."

Diomed waited for him to go on.

"I saw him the other evening beside the Tiber. I stayed to watch. He was preaching and baptizing people in the river, and a vast crowd jammed the banks to listen to him, hanging on his every word and then clamoring and stumbling and pushing each other into the very river to kiss his feet or touch his garment. I was too far away to hear him, but I knew him. Like me, he is becoming an old man now, but I would know him anywhere. I asked the lady Pomponia afterward to tell me of his doings in Rome. It seems he has been here before, many years ago."

He paused a moment and swirled the golden wine in his goblet, as though, looking into it, he would find there his next words.

"She told me he preaches the new religion of the Christus. She said that there are thousands who follow it here in Rome, and many more thousands through all the eastern world. They call themselves Christians. There were twelve men who followed Jesus of Nazareth, and of these Simon Peter is the leader. The leader of the Christians, the teacher of the Word of the Christus; the most important, it seems, of all those who followed him in his life. And this I *do not understand!*"

Loud and bewildered, the last words seemed to be forced out of him, belying all the dignity of his grizzled hair and his military rank, and all the glitter and grandeur of his splendid uniform. The painted room was full of the same intensity of feeling that had filled it when the Greek at last had talked of Galilee, and Gretorix suddenly remembered the night they were recalled to Rome, when his master had talked to Tertius; the cold northern room had grown sharp with the same tension.

The two pairs of boys' eyes were fixed on him, watching

39

him intently, and at last Diomed said timidly, "Understand what, sir?" The Praetor seemed as puzzled and confused as he himself. Justus laid down his crystal glass, and his eyes looked out beyond the pale walls into the past.

"I have seen Peter before. When I was a young tribune in the Antonia in Jerusalem." He stopped again as though he found it difficult to talk. He breathed deeply. "It was the night," he said, "that they took this man Jesus of Nazareth. Preaching sedition was their charge against him. It was nothing to do with us, nothing at all. It was the Temple servants who took him. I was not even on duty that night. But I was curious, for he seemed to me to have done little wrong. They took him to the house of Annas, and there was a vast crowd there, fighting and jostling as if it were a cockfight or a games. I pushed my way out of it and went round to the courtyard to try and get in by another door. In the court there was a fire—it was the time of the Jewish Passover, you know, and the nights were still cold—and I stopped beside it for a moment's warmth. Then this man Peter came in. I would know him anywhere —a huge fellow with a great head of curly hair. He came reeling in as though he could hardly stand. At first I thought him to be drunk, but in the light of the fire I saw him to be half mad with grief. A Galilean, I thought—his grief must be for this man they have taken. He must be a friend of his. And this I *do not* understand. They tell me now he was the leader of them all, the right-hand man of Jesus of Nazareth, and yet, that night beside the fire when he was asked, he swore he knew him not."

Justus' face was no longer that of the commanding soldier of high rank. It was creased with the bewilderment of years, the puzzle that had never left his mind through all the years between.

"He denied him. Twice while I listened. And yet, he suffered for him. I have never seen a man so rage with grief. Then a cock crew, and I knew it to be dawn and I was due on duty. I went away."

He sat with his hands upon his knees, staring into space, and the young Briton looked at Diomed as if he waited for him to speak.

"Were you there," Diomed asked hesitantly after a long time, "when they crucified his friend?"

"Yes." The Praetor answered shortly, and said no more.

Diomed had to press on, risking anger.

"And my lord," he said, "what did you think of him?"

The older man stood up abruptly in a hiss of leather and a swirl of purple cloak, walking sharply until he was brought up by the wall; and there he stood, seemingly intent on the pale, delicate colors of the flying birds, the fine loving detail of an eye, the point of a yellow beak. When he spoke he did not turn around.

"What should I think of him," he said harshly. "What was he to me, or I to him? I was a Roman soldier, my son, a Tribune of noble birth, all my career before me. It was not my place to think."

He turned back as he finished speaking, but his face was drawn and he did not look at either of the boys.

"And Peter?" Diomed pressed. "Was he there when his friend—died?"

"He was not." The voice was curt.

"May I speak, my lord Justus?" Justus looked at the slave and nodded.

"Come round where I can see you," said Diomed urgently, and Gretorix moved to his feet.

"I have heard of all this," he said. "Long, long ago in Britain. From a legionary who was there. He said—"

"Whatever he said, you are better to forget it now that you belong in this house." Justus paced the colored floor, and his face had the same shuttered, almost fearful look Demetrius had worn; as though they faced something too big for understanding that yet drew them, whether they would or no. "The poor Jews," went on Justus with a short laugh. "They gave Jesus of Nazareth to the Romans to crucify, that they might make an end of him. They only made a beginning. Did they not realize that by means of the soldiers who stood below the cross they sent word of him to every farthest corner of the known world—even to Gretorix here in the swamps of his forsaken Britain? For though they might not dare to think of it, like me, there was no man, my sons, who stood below that cross and managed to forget it. Now I must go to the Emperor."

Gretorix sprang to hand him his helmet, burnishing the silver with his sleeve and shaking out the great, dancing purple plumes.

Justus had resumed his calm and authority.

"We have talked in private, my young Diomed, and keep it so. If you value your slave, do not let him babble of the Christus in your father's house. Peter and his Christus preach a kingdom that is above all kingdoms, and that does not go well with those like your father who have ambitions in the kingdom of Rome. I bid you good day. Diomed —look well to your new slave. Gretorix—have care for your new master. He cannot care for himself."

The two boys looked at each other as the sound of his nailed boots grew dim along the colonnade and they lost the sound of his voice calling for his slaves.

"Tell me, Gretorix." Diomed's face was urgent. "Quickly, before anybody else comes. This legionary who told you of the crucifixion of this man. What did he say that my lord Justus would not let you repeat?"

"I am in your father's house."

"It is between us. Come, I command you. No, no—I do not do that. I ask you."

Gretorix glanced at the curtained door.

"My lord Justus knows as well as I what he said."

42

"Well, what did he say!"

"He said that he had fought the whole world over in the Legions of Rome, and had seen many sights more terrible than he could tell, in all the wars. But nothing was carved deeper upon his brain, he said, than the day they crucified this carpenter from Nazareth." Gretorix's Latin was rough and strange, and Diomed frowned to concentrate upon his words. "He said he died around the tenth hour, and yet the sky grew dark as a winter night and the heavens rolled and thundered; the earth split wide open in great gashes, and in the town of Jerusalem the buildings rocked and trembled. It is many years since I have seen this soldier, but always he talked of this; he could not talk enough of it, as though it haunted him. I have never forgotten it. However many times he told it, the story always held me. He said—"

"He said?" Diomed prompted him.

"He said—and this I do not understand. He said that this Jesus of Nazareth was the Son of God. I have heard the Legate Tertius say this also, to my lord."

The Son of God. Diomed remembered the careful face of Demetrius, and the suggestion that he had found what his mother sought. A new God. The true God. His word was being preached now in Rome by Peter down by the Tiber, and in His Name he healed the sick.

"Gretorix—" His eyes were filled with the urgency of purpose his body could not show. "Gretorix, can you find your way about Rome?"

The fair-haired boy drew close, as if he sensed what was in his mind.

"I ran at my lord's stirrup in the time before my lady Pomponia brought me to you. I know a little, and I can manage. I have been long among Romans. What would you have me do?"

"I would have you be my legs, Gretorix. Send me Pallius and Melas to stay with me while you are gone—and above all do not let Xania know, or there will be more tears and trouble, and she will say it only proves how ill you care for me. Go then down into the city, and find for me this old man Simon Peter. Follow him and listen to him. Tell me where he goes and what he does." There was a long moment of silence, and it seemed as if Diomed had to swallow heavily before he could speak again. When he did, his voice was hoarsely casual. "And find out," he added, and did not look at Gretorix, "if what Demetrius says is true. That in the name of Jesus of Nazareth he can heal the sick."

When Xania came fussing in at the appointed time with the dumb, devoted Fuscus flexing his fingers at her heels, Diomed apparently slept. At his head stood Pallius with the great scarlet feather fan, which he waved gently over the boy, against the rising heat.

The new slave, he said with a blank face, had gone on a small errand for his young master.

Chapter 4

While Fuscus rubbed devotedly at the wasted muscles of the sick boy, and Gretorix threaded his careful way through the thronging masses of the city, the Praetor Justus Gallius was received by his Emperor.

"Bid him here," he said, when Justus was announced. "And go away. Go away, all of you. I am sick of you. Think you it suits me, Tigellenus? No—" Some of the slaves moved to clear the litter of his toilet. "No, leave it. Go." He had slept late and was still in his dressing room, which opened from his vast, pillared bedchamber. As the crowd of slaves who barbered and dressed him whispered together and withdrew, Nero peered close into a silver mirror at the tumbling reddish curls of his hair, his dissolute young face pale and ill-tempered. "He has done it well enough," he said, before the tall man who moved round to look at it could answer him.

Tigellenus smoothed his thin, shrewd face into a mask of interest and approval.

"It becomes your Imperial Majesty most excellently." He moved to face the Emperor through the mass of priceless bowls and jeweled basins, ointments and amphorae, fine combs and mirrors, and the clutter of discarded clothes that was Nero's dressing room. He was not in his uniform as Captain of the Praetorian Guard, but fresh and immaculate in a spotless white toga bordered with the purple of a Senator. The Emperor eyed him sourly, and his heavy, irritable eyes were bloodshot and weary.

"You are always up so *early*, Tigellenus, my friend," he said disagreeably. "Always so clean and wide awake. You must have a good barber, and I must watch, must I not, lest someday you get up too early for *me*."

Tigellenus spoke carefully.

"I am your Imperial Majesty's most faithful and loyal servant."

"Hm! Does such a thing exist?" Nero got up from his carved silver chair and walked with small, mincing steps across the room. His legs under the royal tunic were white and sticklike, seemingly too frail to carry the weight of gems that gleamed in his sandal straps. On a gilded table, a great enameled bowl of white narcissus threw the fragrance of spring against the heavy perfumes of the room. He took one and held it to his face.

"Ah," he said, breathing deeply. "It tells me the summer is almost come and we will leave this hot city, full of evil, for the peace of the hills and the sweet silence of Capri.

Have I even *one* loyal servant, Tigellenus?" The question was thrown so sharply through the flower before his face that for a moment the smooth urbanity of Tigellenus was confused. He had been listening to the Emperor's words about the sweet peace and silence, and thinking that the whole world knew that the summer palaces, free from the unavoidable tasks of Rome, were the scenes of orgies more wild and terrible than any the Imperial Palace on the Quirinal could know. The sudden, sharp question about loyalty threw him off his balance, and only the appearance of Justus saved him.

"Here is one, I am sure, Imperial Caesar," he said, indicating Justus in the doorway. "The Praetor Justus Gallius, late Commander of the Legions in Britain, and now come, you will remember, to share with me the honor of the command of your Guard."

The nails of the soldier's boots clicked on the white marble floor as he moved forward to salute his Emperor, and his disciplined campaigner's eyes flicked with disgust and amazement round the perfumed, littered room; it was scattered idly and carelessly with wealth that could pay a legion. The sharp, narrow eyes of Tigellenus saw his disgust with pleasure. Nero could not have helped him better than by receiving this rigid old soldier in his dressing room! But Nero thought only of himself, the white flower between his fingertips, his shallow mind leaping from one thing to the next.

"Ah, yes. You are long away from Rome, Justus Gallius. We have not seen you before. Handsome—yes. And tall. I approve, Tigellenus—he will look well behind me on State occasions. Good. Well, you may take wine with me, Justus Gallius, on your appointment. Tigellenus, my toga."

Tigellenus snapped his fingers to the Emperor's dresser, who folded his small, awkward figure into the depths of the Imperial toga, and Justus bit back his temper and watched, impassive. His Emperor was still a young man, but he had heard tell that the old Egyptians had a saying that the names of the gods men worshiped were written large upon their faces. And on the still young face of Nero, the names that were written were those of vanity and greed, cruelty and self-indulgence, and selfishness. A dangerous master, close at hand.

He followed as Nero strutted through the pillared archways, and the spears of his Guards ground on the marble floors as he passed. In a small withdrawing room, banked with the treasures of the Empire, Justus was waved to the silken cushions of a copper couch deep laid with gold; before him was a table mosaicked with the leaping maidens of the old Greeks. A trail of slaves padded in on soft feet with cups of solid gold.

The Emperor reached for his cup, and then drew back, his bloodshot eyes sour on the slave who held it.

"Where is Xanthus?" he said querulously. "Where is my cupbearer?"

The captain of the group moved forward, and his clasped hands were trembling. It was enough to cost him his head that the Emperor's favorite cupbearer had dared to die. He blinked at the inlaid floor and begged his gods to protect him.

"Dead?" said Nero indignantly after he had spoken. He raised himself on his elbow and his hot eyes under the tumbling curls were furious on the trembling slave. "How dared he? Did he have my permission to die?"

There was silence in the gorgeous room, broken only by the hoarse, anxious breathing of the slave, and Justus and Tigellenus looked carefully into their cups. Tigellenus could have cried with pleasure to see his Emperor so betray himself. Nero scolded and grumbled, and in the end he petulantly waved the slaves away and turned to his guests.

48

When he had at last dismissed them also, they walked together through the corridors of the cool, airy Palace, moving from the gilded pillars, the inlaid floors, the flowers, the fountains, and the priceless treasures of a plundered world into the plainer quarters where the Praetorian Guard were lodged on duty. Daily, in their pomp and glory, they marched backward and forward to their barracks on the Via Tiburtina.

"Come with me to my office, Justus," said Tigellenus with great show of familiarity, and Justus shot him a glance of surprise. But Tigellenus was his senior officer, and so he turned and followed him without comment, through the echoing armories where the long spears stood shining in their ranks in the wooden racks, and sun through the high windows splintered on the massed curves of greave and breastplate.

The room of Tigellenus was large, bare and military looking, and Justus glanced round approvingly at the table with its scrolls and papers neatly piled, and the maps and charts of the city which hung on the walls. Tigellenus bade the soldier at the door to see they were not disturbed, and he motioned Justus to a bench, sitting down opposite him and surveying him through his bright, narrow eyes as though he waited for an opening. Justus gave him no help. Placing his plumed helmet on the bench beside him, he waited in easy silence for his superior to speak.

"Well, my friend," Tigellenus said at last. "Now you have met our Emperor." His colorless eyes never left the other man's face, bright with expectancy.

"Yes." Justus was carefully expressionless, but the hair on the back of his neck pricked him a warning of danger, and his calves twitched as they had always done when the legions were lined for battle, and he must drop his hand to give the signal for attack. Tigellenus moved in his chair and tried again.

49

"Do you know, Justus Gallius, just why you are brought back to Rome?" he asked. His face was full of amiable friendliness.

"Well, yes, sir," answered Justus with great simplicity. "I have been told that I am to act under you in command of the Guard for a time, and to take full command when you are given another post."

"Another post," mused Tigellenus. "Yes, that will do to describe it. Another post. You are a first-class soldier, Justus. You have commanded the legions now in Germany and Gaul, and have been in full command in Britain. Wherever the name of Justus Gallius is mentioned to the troops, they speak of him among the gods. I have no doubt that the Guard will soon have the same feeling."

"Sir, you do me too much honor." Justus was stiff. He could not see where this was leading, but he was too old a goose to be cooked with flattery. And he did not like the cunning look beneath the smooth, amiable mask on the other man's face.

"No, indeed." The Captain's voice was a little less certain, and he played among the parchments on his table, his eyes flickering up to Justus and then down again to his restless hands. Ah, thought Justus, now we come to the meat on the bone, and unless I am much mistaken, the meat is bad.

"You have all the army at your back, Justus Gallius. That is a position of great power. If there should be a—shall we say a change of power in Rome, and you supported it, then all the army would support it also, for they are yours to a legionary. This would give the new Emp— the new authority great security."

Justus' eyes snapped open wide in his tanned face as he stared across the table in anger and disbelief. Had he been brought all the way across the world with promise of promotion, merely to be used in some plot against the Emperor—dissolute, poor wretch though he may be? Coldly he looked at Tigellenus and put his thoughts into words.

"Have I been brought back to Rome, sir, only to help you in some scheme to kill Nero Caesar?"

Tigellenus spread his hands and lifted his narrow shoulders.

"No. No. Not to kill him, Justus. Not to kill him. With a little care and planning we could see that the people of Rome would do that themselves. They murmur enough against him already, and we could find a way of fixing guilt for some disaster that would outrage them. And with the army at the back of the new Emperor, nothing could go wrong. There would be a great future for you in this."

"I see." Justus got up and crossed to the window, looking down absently over the cypressed gardens of the rich and the packed tenements of the Murcia valley, the great sandstone arches of the Circus Maximus and, over to his right, the pale, gleaming curve of the Tiber. His tone was icy.

"May I be permitted to ask the name of the proposed new Emperor?"

There was silence behind him, and he looked back. Tigellenus had bent his head and was examining his nails. There was a faint flush on his face and a look of pride that was almost foolish. Justus looked at him in distaste.

"I see. That was the 'new post' you spoke of." He turned and looked down again over Rome. How often in the gray, damp days in the northern countries he had thought of this scene—looking out over the sodden, shapeless trees and the mist-wreathed fields with his mind longing for the sharp darkness of cypresses in gardens pale with roses and crisp with the smell of herbs, the air clear and luminous and the sun on the distant Tiber. Now it soured and sickened in his throat. He had no more use than Tigellenus for the warped young creature who now held great

Caesar's throne; but there were other ways than murder. And not even an honest killing, but some base trick to hand the responsibility to the citizens of Rome. It was no place for a soldier, or his men, to lend a hand to so shoddy a plot. He turned sharply to his superior.

"I have no part in it," he said harshly. "I take up my duties tomorrow as I am posted. To Imperial Caesar's bodyguard, for the *protection* of his Majesty and the city of Rome." He took his helmet from where he had laid it down, and stood formally before Tigellenus.

"Have you any further orders for me, sir?"

The face of Tigellenus had grown shrunken and ugly, all urbanity gone, its native meanness underlined by the extreme neatness and cleanliness of his clothes and grooming.

"Only this, my proud Justus Gallius," he said, and his voice was sharp with malice. "Only this. I do not ask favors twice, and you have lost your chance. And if one word leaks out of what I have said today, then you are a dead man. Who would believe you against me? Remember, I am not without power, even as I am." He drew himself up. "Remember," he said, and realized his words too late, "I am the Emperor's best friend."

There was a long pause, and Justus could not let it go.

"So I observe, my lord Tigellenus," he answered bitingly. "So I observe." He knew he was unwise, and it was small satisfaction to watch the ugly flush creep up the face of Tigellenus. As he saluted formally and turned to leave, he knew that he had made a dangerous enemy.

A good morning's work, he thought ruefully as he passed down the marble steps between the crashing spears of the guards, and his slaves ran to meet him with his horse. A good morning's work. He looked back at the marble masses of the Imperial Palace. Within one hour he had found there for himself a mad, dangerous master and a deadly enemy. Ah, well—Tertius had warned him of this before he ever came.

He sighed and slowly mounted his horse in the forecourt of the Palace. His servants fell in to run behind him, and he turned toward the crowded bustle of the Forum, to cross it and go on up toward the house of Aulus Plautius and Pomponia, peaceful on the heights of the Viminal. Suddenly, in the middle of the Forum's midday turmoil, he pulled on his studded reins, and paused and thought a moment. The anger and concern left his eyes. He circled the great golden milestone that marked the center of the world, and changed his direction, threading downhill through the crowds of fashionable Tuscan Street toward the Tiber.

When the river was close, and the large, rich shops giving place to the packed tenements and the booths of the smaller traders, he paused again, realizing suddenly the conspicuous figure he made in this poorer quarter where the small wooden houses tilted over the crowded streets, and the frail, ill-built tenements towered in perpetual danger of collapse. The crowds who pressed back along the walls to give the Praetor passage raised startled faces to the plumes and glory of his uniform, and counted in amazement the puzzled slaves who followed him. Only tardily was he aware of this, his mind fixed on the purpose that drew him to the river.

"Here!" He stopped and dismounted, and handed the reins to the slave who ran at his stirrup. "Take the horse, and lead it home. I will not need it again." Before the quick-gathering, ever-curious Roman crowd, he took off his bright helmet and beckoned his slaves to unbuckle him from his burnished armor. Smiling slightly at their dismayed, astonished faces, he dismissed them all and bade them take it home. He eased his body in the cool looseness of his tunic, and ran his hands through his graying hair where the sweat was banded from the lining of his heavy helmet. He moved calmly through the whispering, curious crowd and on alone toward the river.

Peter was preaching on the other side of the bridge; the crowds packed around him in the narrow space between the water and the tumbling, huddled poverty of the district of Transtiberium, the last haven of the wretched, and the haunt and dwelling place of the pauper, the criminal, and the destitute. It was almost noon—the high, hot noon of Rome, when the people sought the shade and gathered by the cool pleasure of the fountains. But this crowd was gathered in the full sun, indifferent, their rapt, exalted faces turned toward the elderly man who stood upon a pile of stones close by the bridge. It was the same man. Justus grew more certain each time he saw him. His mind went back to the reeling giant, sick with grief, who had denied his Master across the fire in the courtyard of Annas. The man was older, the great head of dark curls grown sparse and gray above the still bushy beard. The massive, restless body was quiet now, with the stillness of authority, and the deep voice that spoke to the silent crowds was firm and measured. Petrus, thought the watching man. The Rock. He is well-named, whoever named him. He has that quality.

Suddenly he was filled with an urgent and desperate desire to hear what he was saying that could hold these faces rapt and still, oblivious to the midday heat. But even the steps down from the bridge were crammed with listening people, piled one upon the other in all the stench and squalor of their poverty, Jew and Gentile mixed together, here and there, strangely, the soft colors and fine clothes of the rich; all so intent on what they strained to hear that they barely noticed the thrust and push of the man

54

who inched his way closer, grown suddenly desperate to be in reach.

Slowly he edged his way down, heedless of the rasp of bare legs and arms on the rough stones of the bridge, and sick with a dismay he did not understand when he reached the riverbank only to see Peter bless the crowds and rise to move away. He blinked, to try to calm the violence of his feelings. He was not young, and he had not felt such disappointment in time he could remember; violence and impulsiveness were subdued in his life by discipline. He struggled to remember he was middle-aged and a Praetor; he must not fight and shout and struggle to reach the tall, heavy figure that moved away through the crowd. He stood where he was, and sweat beaded on his forehead and sick disappointment welled in him like a tide of misery.

The people did not have his patience. They would not let Peter go, struggling and crowding and thrusting round him, desperate to kiss his hands and feet or touch the fold of his robe.

Justus was swept along the riverbank, losing sight of Peter save for the top of his gray head, helpless to move any way except at the will of the fierce press of people round him, gasping for breath in the crush of unwashed bodies in the heat. He used all his height and strength to keep Peter in view, giving way in the end to the same strange urgency that filled all the crowd—to be near him, to speak with him, to touch him.

"My lord Justus." The voice was muffled, half strangled, coming from somewhere below Justus, filled with amazement. "My lord Justus! What are you doing here?" Frantically Gretorix fought his way through a forest of stumbling legs that had brought him to the ground, and Justus hauled him to his feet beside him, panting and disheveled, his fair curls damp with sweat, and the bruises of sandal heels already rising on his face. For a moment he could not speak. Then, "What do you here, my lord?" he said again.

Justus glanced hopelessly across the milling crowd to where the seething core was all now that could show where Peter was.

"I was—curious," he said briefly.

"My young master sent me." Gretorix talked as best he could, shouting above the murmurous hum of the crowd and struggling to keep close to Justus in the pull and thrust of the mass of people. "My young lord sent me to find this Simon Peter, to find if it were true—" He gasped and staggered in a fresh wild surge of the crowd. "What is it? What has happened?"

The steady murmur of the crowd had risen to a higher note, shrill and wild with wonder, and the seething center broke apart, piling and pressing back to form an avenue. Through it a woman ran and stumbled, tears pouring down a face that was mad with joy. In her arms a small, bewildered boy blinked and screwed up his wide eyes to look at the hot, blue sky. Through the parting crowd she ran for the bridge and the quiet of her home, and behind her the people closed again, silent now, whispering of what they had seen.

"The child!" Word passed from one to the next. "The child," they whispered, "was born blind. It had never seen. Peter laid a hand upon its head, and now it sees."

Gretorix forgot he was a slave. He gripped Justus' arm with both his hands, and his blue eyes were dark and wide.

"My lord Justus," he whispered hoarsely. "My young master bade me come here to find if it were true that in his Master's name Peter could heal the sick." Justus looked at him and shook his head in silence.

When they turned again to look for Peter he was gone—vanished without trace from the murmuring crowd.

As the golden shadows of the Roman evening crept into the painted room, Gretorix told his young lord of all he had seen that morning by the Tiber. Diomed listened in silence, his eyes fixed on the deepening blue of the sky beyond the windows. When his slave finished speaking, he turned back to look at him, and his eyes were desperate with the confusion of hope at once gained and lost.

"And if it is so?" he asked, and his voice was empty. "If it is true that he can heal the sick, what use is it to me? How can I get to him, or he to me? I am a prisoner, and he a Christian. He would not be allowed in my father's house. We cannot reach each other."

"My lord Diomed." Gretorix's square face was creased with the effort to be clear. "My lord Diomed, I listened a long time today to Peter. I got very close to him." He smiled slightly. "His Latin is like mine, a little rough. But this I did understand. He is only here to preach the word of his Master, Jesus of Nazareth. Everything he is and does, he says, is by the power of his God. And he says again what I heard that soldier say so long ago in Britain. That Jesus of Nazareth was the Son of God."

"Well?"

"Well—I think I understood. It is not Peter who heals the sick. It is his God who heals through him."

"So? Am I any nearer to this God than I am to Peter?"

Gretorix stumbled on, confused and excited by the first contact with some great mystery whose edges he had only begun to grasp.

"Peter told a story today of Jesus of Nazareth."

"Quickly, Gretorix. Demetrius is coming. The pediment waits, and he is long late already."

"He told a story of a town that Jesus walked through—I can't remember the name. But in this town there was a Centurion who had a beloved servant who was very sick. Like you. But this Roman soldier had such belief in Jesus

57

that he came out of the barracks and threw himself at his feet. It was not needed, he said, that Jesus should come into his house—he was not worth the honor. Jesus need only say the word, and his servant would be cured. And he was; Jesus said he had not found such faith in all Israel. It is Jesus who heals, even now, through Peter. And I still do not quite understand, but I think you need not really be close to either. The sick servant was not."

Diomed looked at him for a long time.

"Think you this is true?" he said at last.

"It is true." Demetrius stood inside the door, his sandaled feet unheard. Both pairs of eyes turned on him, wide and startled.

"It is true. I saw it happen. In the small town of Capernaum on the Lake of Galilee. Somehow I could not concentrate on the frescoes of Herod Antipas, and for a while I followed Jesus. I was there when the Centurion came."

For a while he was silent, staring into the gathering dusk, seeing again the small white town on the lakeshore. He smelled the dust and heat, and the blown fragrance of oranges as the dry wind rustled through the tamarisks. He heard the rising murmur of the crowd and saw the dark head of the Roman, prostrate in the dust before the lilac fringes of the Master's robe. Lord, he had cried, I am not worthy that Thou shouldst enter under my roof!

"Faith, my young lord," Demetrius said. "Faith is what the Roman had."

"Faith? What is faith? I don't understand. I believe your story, Demetrius, but it still seems to me that if I am to hope at all, I am closer where I am to Peter than I am to his God. And even that," he added hopelessly, "is not close enough."

"Was Peter there?" he asked suddenly, after a long pause. "In Cap— in this town where it happened?"

"Yes." The sculptor looked at the shadows deepening in

the room and threw the cloth back over the head. "I am too late to work today. Yes, Simon Peter was in Capernaum. And by that time he laughed no more. He was the first follower of Jesus."

Along the shadowed colonnade grew the hiss and swish of sandals, and Mancus the Steward came in with his train of slaves to light the lamps, the spit and flicker of their torches filling the room with red, dancing light. He did not speak, his shrewd black eyes flickering round the silence in the room. The lamps lit, he bowed formally to Diomed and ushered out his slaves; his last sharp glance was for Demetrius.

Chapter 5

"So you know, Pomponia." Justus sat and stared down at his clasped hands between his knees, and the shadows of the trees grew long across the rose beds in the vast peristyle of Pomponia's house.

Pomponia's smile was rueful, and gently she shook her black-veiled head. "Yes, my dear Justus. I know. And so does all Rome."

Justus looked at her sharply.

"How could they not? For an old soldier and a man of your age, I think you have shown little sense. I can only think that you have been so long away from cities, you have forgotten how to live in one. Even though you laid aside your uniform, how *could* it escape the curious eyes of Rome that the Praetor Justus Gallius, newcome to the Imperial Guard, leaves his barracks for every hour that he can spare to follow Peter down among the hovels of the Tiber? I myself did not hear it until yesterday, as my daughter has been sick, and I have stayed close at home with her. So I did not hear all I might."

"Petronilla?" Justus' eyebrows lifted in concern.

"She grows better." Pomponia answered his unspoken question. "But now I will tell you something of her which I would not have told you before. But now, Justus," she turned and laid a hand on his, "now I think you will join us. I must tell you that my Petronilla is the spiritual daughter of Simon Peter himself. He baptized her when he was last in Rome and she was still a child. He is devoted to her. There is nothing he will not do for her.

It was Justus' turn to smile at her.

"It is not the secret you thought, Pomponia, my dear. I heard it in Britain, brought there with all the other gossip of Rome. But Petronilla is married to the Prefect of Rome."

"Exactly, Justus, exactly. That is why I beg you to be careful—you see, the gossip goes to the ends of the world. And as you say, Petronilla is married to the Chief Magistrate of Rome—the right hand of the Emperor, who must do as the Emperor bids him. And the Emperor hates the Christians. Oh, it is a delicate and dangerous thing for such as us, Justus. We must walk two paths at once, lest we endanger those we love. That is why I would have warned you, had I known, that there are other ways for public figures like yourself to follow Peter and hear his teaching. And to be baptized also—if that is what you wish."

Justus looked long over the low marble wall across the golden evening city; it was spiked dark with cypress on the hillsides, and tall groves of tamarisk grew against the sheen of marble, above the haze of huddled houses in the valleys. His mind raced across the hours of words that he had listened to in these last days, in the crowds that pressed round Peter; across the spiteful threats of a thwarted Tigellenus, and the unstable favor of his Emperor; across the promise of glory of his new appointment, and the risk he ran to lose everything if he turned to follow the Christus. Always, as it had never ceased to do, it came back in the end to that blinding day, long, long ago, when he had stood in the roaring darkness below a cross outside Jerusalem. He turned to Pomponia and his face was peaceful.

"Yes," he said. "If Peter finds me worthy, that is what I wish."

"Well, then, come tomorrow evening just after dusk to the house of Cornelius Pudens on the Viminal. I shall be there. Now go carefully, Justus, I beg you. When someone falls from a high place, they are apt to drag down many others with them."

Through these days, Diomed was restless, tossing in his mind as he could not toss in his helpless body, begging Gretorix to repeat over and over again every single thing he had seen or heard, brooding on what the Greek had told him. He lay wide-eyed and fretful through the rising heat of long sleepless nights, and his thin face grew white and weary. The lady Gallia was annoyed, sweeping irritably into his room on her way to her silk merchant or perfumiers, or dressed and painted for some Imperial function. She was forever in a hurry and annoyed that he should claim attention. At her heels Xania fussed and grumbled in self-righteousness, and urged her to lay the blame for her young lord's state where it belonged—on the new slave. He should be sent back, she pressed, where he came from, and the boy given back into her care.

Diomed would have no suggestion of his leaving him. If

it were only mentioned, he grew feverish and wild, so that once more his mother withdrew in despair, giving him his own way and taking Xania with her.

"There," said Diomed when they were gone, and blew out a long, weary sigh. "That battle is won again for the moment. Now Gretorix—" His voice took on a new strength and urgency. "Now they are both safe away, I can let you go again. I did not dare, through all this womens' fuss. Go down again, Gretorix. Find Peter for me again. Listen. Tell me everything. I have the strangest feeling that if I can know more of him, then I will be closer." He did not add his burning hope that if only he could draw close enough, he might be healed.

Gretorix needed no second bidding. Since the last day when he had struggled from the crowd in silence, by the side of Justus, he had been as restless as his young master with his longing to go again.

The shadows were turning from gold to purple in the valleys between the Seven Hills as he slipped out the slaves' entrance of the Villa Verius, and set off at a trot down the steep slopes of the Esquiline. He made at once for the place where he had heard Simon Peter preach before, threading his way through the crowds that still thronged the open spaces of the Forum in the lingering light, and plunging on downward through the streets of shuttered shops that narrowed toward the Tiber. Peter was not there.

When he came panting to the edges of the river, the far bank was empty save for a pack of screeching urchins who dipped and scrambled in the shallows by the bridge, where the water held the sinking sun and their pale bodies dripped with gold. Gretorix halted. He had no idea where to go to search for him. The last day, he had found him just by chance, and for all his brave words to Diomed, he had small idea of the maze of Rome. The few days he had run at Justus' stirrup had done little more than confuse him. Without purpose, he turned back up the hill toward the Forum, for instinct told him it would not be wise, with the badge of Verius Bautus on his tunic, to betray himself to strangers by asking the whereabouts of Peter. Unhappily he faced the thought of going back to his young master with nothing more to tell.

In the silent dusk of the narrow street, where the tilting houses closed across the sky, he heard clearly the lisp of sandal straps behind him, and looked idly at the man who passed him, walking quickly, holding close against the shuttered shops, as though he sought the deepest shadows. The boy's eyes snapped open suddenly in hope. He could not see well, but he was sure he knew him. He quickened his pace to stay close behind, stumbling along in darkness on the unpaved street. The man ahead moved quickly and decisively—uphill. He knew where he was going.

At the foot of Tuscan Street, where the road widened into the fashionable shopping streets, they were halted together at a junction, held by a squad of fire watchers marching to their night's posts. They passed in the reek and hiss of pitch from their flaring torches, and in the brief flickering light, Gretorix snatched a glance at the man who had paused beside him, a slightly younger man than Peter himself, with a mild, withdrawn face. The boy suppressed a cry of triumph. Undoubtedly it was the man who had been beside him that last day on Tiber bank, who sat below him with tablets in his hands and wrote down the slow, deep words that Peter spoke, then put aside his writing and drew protectively to his side as the press of the crowd grew great.

Quick with excitement Gretorix followed him again when the fire watchers had passed and left the street in darkness. Once more he threaded the chattering, crowded Forum, alive now with the glare and spit of torches, desperate lest he lose sight of his man in the mill of people.

He sighed with relief when they went on upward through the poorer streets, which gave way in turn to the wide, paved roads along the summit of a hill, and the blank, white walls of the great houses of the rich. Behind them lay the city in its valleys, and the dark hills all round were pricked with lights. Screwing up his eyes against the darkness, Gretorix thought he could make out the dark shape of the Esquiline across the valley, and the white ghostly masses of the Villa Verius.

So suddenly that the boy was taken by surprise, the man stopped at one of the vast doors that reared their torchlit splendor in the marble walls along the street. As Gretorix slipped abruptly into the shadows behind him, he knocked, and in an instant a small door opened in the large one, and he stepped inside. But not before the boy so close behind him had heard the one word spoken to the servant at the door.

"Christus," he had said.

Hesitant, the boy waited in the shadows beyond the torchlit gate, his eyes roving hopelessly over the high walls, wondering what he should do. Impossible to climb, yet he felt certain that somewhere behind them he would find all he searched for. Even as he watched, another man came quietly and knocked on the bronze gate.

"Christus," he said, also in a whisper, and was gone.

And then two women.

Gretorix seized his courage. He did not know by now whether he did this for Diomed or for himself. But he must find out all he could. He moved over and stood before the great gate. The sheen of bronze rose high above his head, and beneath his hand were panels of chalcedony and onyx. On the small door, the knocker was strangely in the shape of a golden fish. He breathed deeply and knocked as the others had done. The small gate opened instantly, and through it looked the formless face of a man who stared from light to darkness.

"Christus," said Gretorix firmly, and tried to still the unsteady thumping of his heart. He moved a little sideways from the stream of warm golden light that flowed from behind the man and out the open door. But with no word spoken, the man moved back and opened the door wider. Gretorix stepped through.

He stood in a large, richly furnished atrium, but to his anxious mind it was nothing but a confusion of soft golden light and silken couches, gleaming pillars and gaily colored floor, massed flowers and the quick whisper of falling water. He did not dare to pause even for a moment under the eyes of the doorkeeper. The atrium was empty, and he set out as steadily as he could across the gorgeous floor, stiffening the trembling of his knees, and hearing nothing but the thudding of his own giant heart. With every step he waited for the call that would bring him back to question his slave's tunic and his very presence in this great house. But no call came, and, sick with relief, he passed through the archways at the other end and found himself out in the pillared spaces of the peristyle. He leaned against a wall and caught his breath.

The first stars pricked out above him in the lambent purple of the sky, and the air was heavy with the massed perfume of the flowers, and sharpened by the tang of the fresh earth, new watered after the hot day by the slaves of the garden. Steadier, he eased himself off his wall and began to walk carefully and quietly round the colonnaded walks, where the climbing roses plucked at his hair in the darkness, and on the ground flowers brushed and tickled at his ankles and threw their disturbed perfume up into the warm night. He was attracted by a long row of lighted windows on the far side of the peristyle. When at last he reached them, he could find no outer door—only the taunting glow

66

of the unshuttered windows well above his head and the soft murmur of voices, men's and women's, clear in the silent garden.

He looked around him. The vast terra-cotta pots of flowering shrubs, half as high as himself, might have been placed there with thought for him alone. Carefully he pulled himself up the smooth, rounded surface until he could place his feet firmly in the earth around the plants and stand up. His chin rested on the sill of one of the windows, and he had a clear view of the room inside.

He was just in time to see the man whom he had followed come in through the red-curtained door, and his mouth and eyes fell open wide to see that it was the lady Pomponia who moved across the floor to greet him.

"Mark," she said. She bent her black-veiled head and held out her two hands. "We were afraid something had happened to you. You are late."

The man laid down his scrolls and tablets on a side table.

"Forgive me, Lucina. Nothing has happened. I was writing and forgot the hour."

Gretorix's face creased in perplexity. Pomponia? Lucina? Why did the lady Pomponia have two names?

His astonishment increased as he turned his eyes to the rest of the big room. Down the center of it ran a long, plain table made of wood, and on its bare top a simple meal was laid—nothing but jugs of wine and cups, and loaves of bread in rush baskets. What a meal for so rich a house! In the center of the long table was the vast form of Peter, presiding, overflowing his chair in the folds of his garments, his gray head bent, incredibly, to listen to the words of the Praetor Justus Gallius, who had the place of honor to his left. A little farther down the table, the boy saw the sculptor Demetrius, and beside him the young lady Petronilla, whose serene, exquisite beauty he had seen once, and never forgotten, in the house of Pomponia. Many, many more were there, ranged along the plain wooden table, and Gretorix saw with amazement that most of their togas had the purple stripe of rank. There were two places empty, for the lady Pomponia and the friend of Peter whom she had called Mark. When they were seated, the simple meal began.

Gretorix watched spellbound, understanding nothing, held by he knew not what, feeling again this sense of awe and mystery that had first touched him so long ago in the rough and anguished storytelling of the soldier in far Britain. First the company about the table seemed to pray, Peter speaking and they answering in Latin too soft and swift for the boy to understand. Then they sat again to the table, but before they ate, Peter turned slowly and laid his hands on the broad shoulders of Justus, and leaning, he kissed him. Justus turned then to Mark upon his left, and he in turn to his neighbor, and so on down to the end of the table.

Peter then laid his great brown fisherman's hands in the basket of bread before him. Taking some, he broke it, and raised his head to speak. His eyes were turned up toward the watching boy, and there was in them some expression that made Gretorix on the instant close his own, and try to bend his head.

He moved too suddenly. Beneath him, the earth gave way, and with a thunderous crash the jar went over and he sprawled on the ground in a welter of spilled earth and shattered terra-cotta and crumpled flowers.

There had been no sight or sound of watchmen in the peristyle. Now they were on him in a flash, dragging him away with kicks and cuffs, and refusing to allow him to say anything of what he did. Dodging a kick as he was hustled through the back corridors of the house, Gretorix groaned and cursed himself for a fool. This new young master of his had caught his pity. He would do anything to help him, but now what use would he be to him, lodged in a felon's jail?

He shouted again at his captors, but they took no heed, tightening their grip on him and hustling him along even more roughly. Only when he was dragged before the Steward of the House in the cluttered room of his office would anybody listen to him.

"I meant no harm!" he shouted again at the man who stood behind the table. The shadows of the torchlight reared vast behind him in the vaulted room, and the unsteady light fell on the long rows of monstrous keys, the piles of scrolls, and the neatly stacked tablets—all the records and organization of a great house. "I meant no harm! I only wanted to *see!* The lady Pomponia will tell you who I am, or the Praetor Justus Gallius. They will know of me!"

"To whose house do you belong?" The round, steady face of the Steward was firm and competent, his shrewd dark eyes flicking over the furious boy, his thumbs hooked in the wide leather of his belt. "Ah!" His eyebrows lifted as he saw the badge on the front of the earth-stained tunic. "Verius Bautus? Strange."

Gretorix shook at the hands that held him, and the Steward signed to the watchmen to let him stand alone.

Gretorix struggled for his breath.

"I am owned by the lady Pomponia, but she has given me into the service of the young lord Diomed, the crippled son of the Senator Verius."

The Steward continued to eye him, looking curiously at the long, fair hair and the sunburned skin.

"What is your country?"

The boy raised his head proudly.

"Britain."

"Hm! The edge of the world. Are you a Christian?"

For some reason the sudden question confused Gretorix, filling him with a storm of feeling and excitement that he did not understand, bringing back the overwhelming moment when he had met the lifted eyes of Peter. His answer, when he gave it, surprised him.

"I don't know!" he blurted out, gazing at the calm, round-faced man in bewilderment.

"I am," answered the Steward quietly. "So are all who serve in this house. That was why I was surprised to see you here with the house badge of the Senator Verius, who does not have Christians as his slaves. You can go," he added to the watchmen. "Leave him here. Sit there boy, and wait. When they are ready to go, I will speak to the Praetor and the lady Lucina and see if what you say is true."

"Lucina" again. Why Lucina? Gretorix subsided on to the bench, sore from his fall and the beating he had got afterward, too confused and puzzled for one night to ask any more questions.

It was Justus himself to whom he was brought later, in the atrium, a strangely quiet, exalted Justus who seemed oddly pleased that the boy had seen what he had, and took him gladly in his charge. He bade him run at his stirrup until their ways parted.

"And do you know?" Late that night, when the household of Verius was long asleep, Gretorix was still crouched beside Diomed's bed, and the two boys whispered together in the warm darkness. "Do you know where I was? Where I saw all this?" Gretorix's voice was still filled with amazement.

"Where?"

"In the house of a Senator. On that hill across the valley there—The one called the Viminal. His name is Cornelius Pudens—is that right?"

"Yes. He is known to my father."

"Well, he may be, but he is a Christian, and so is his

lady. It is in their house that Peter lives, and also Mark, another of the first twelve, who is his scribe." Gretorix was tumbling and thrashing through all his new knowledge, gained as he ran beside Justus through the silent streets along the hilltop. "It is there the Christians gather and listen to the teaching of Peter. And it does not matter who you are in the sight of the Christus—slave and Senator sit down together. That is why the doorman took no heed of me in my slave's tunic. And my lord Justus said that the next time I go he hopes it may be through the door to sit with him and all the others at this table."

"Why is the table so important?"

"It is not. It is the meal that matters. They do it in memory of the last supper of Jesus of Nazareth on the night before his crucifixion, when he gathered his twelve around him for a meal. And he washed their feet and kissed them, and so they kiss each other now with the kiss of peace. And he broke bread and drank wine, and bade them do it always in memory of him. And so his followers gather Christians round them now, and do as he bade them—love feasts, they call these gatherings. There are many, my lord said, in Rome, but secret, lest they attract too much attention."

He paused for breath, dazed with the amount that he had learned that night of a strange, unknown world that drew him in awe and excitement.

"It is to one of these feasts," he said after a pause, "that my lord Justus said he will bring me."

Diomed's mind roamed over all he had been told, growing frantic at the sense of some great and urgent mystery growing round him, whose knowledge would be forever beyond his grasp.

"Well, what," he burst out in all his misery and frustration, "is there to hold you back? You have legs."

For a long time there was no sound but the disturbed

breathing of the unhappy boy and, from the gardens below them on the hill, the rapturous welcome of a nightingale to summer.

Then Gretorix did a thing which, as a slave, could earn him death. He laid a hand unasked upon his master. His grip was cool and firm on the inert arm of the paralyzed boy, but his voice when he spoke was tense with wonder.

"Because," he said, "I would need first to be baptized. I don't know if I am ready."

Chapter 6

The warm, sweet spring lengthened into the burning days of high summer, when the skies hung brazen above the sweating streets of Rome, and in the colonnaded peristyles of the great houses, the scent of flowers lay heavy as a burden on the hot, dry air. Down in the city, the people gathered at the fountains and searched for air along the shrinking reaches of the Tiber, and at the Pond of Agrippa in the Ninth District, the loyal Tigellenus spread a banquet for his Divine Master, to prove his devotion with a glory that would outshine the greatest Circus.

Over the small lake, edged with the dark greenery of sacred groves and the pale glimmer of marble temples, a vast floating platform was erected to hold the brilliant stripes of tents and awnings, the fluting and fringes of pavilions and porticoes. Handpicked slaves strutted and prinked at the ribbons in their long, scented hair and impudently jangled the deep rows of golden bracelets at their wrists and ankles. Below ceilings looped with fresh-cut flowers, they set the marble tables with the sheen of gold and the sharp glitter of spangled crystal.

Nero was pleased. He minced to his ivory couch, blinking his protuberant red-lashed eyes in pleasure, and the torchlight caught the glint of gold dust in his hair. From Africa, for his amusement, Tigellenus had brought elephants and tigers, wolves and bears from the hills of Scythia, and strange, enormous turtles from the hot, sandy shores of the far south. The chains of their captivity were wreathed in flowers, and their wild, sullen eyes glared out resentfully through loops of scented garlands.

As darkness fell, hundreds of torches flared across the lake, filling the gaudy platform with their brilliance, and with choirs and music the revels raced along. Guests staggered to the lakeside to ease themselves in sickness that they might stagger back to eat and drink again. From the banks of the lake, Rome watched in silence the public orgies of their Emperor, and even when Nero himself seized his lyre and stumbled uncertainly to sing to them at the edge of the torchlit waters, they could raise no more than dutiful applause.

In the place of honor at Nero's left hand, Tigellenus, his friend, reclined in satisfaction, smiling his narrow, secret smile, beckoning constantly to the slaves whose place it was to fill the Emperor's cup, and prompting him to every indiscretion his small mind could think of which could disgrace an Emperor on this blazing public island under the watching eyes of his people.

Farther down the table, Justus Gallius watched them both, moving his crystal cup aside from the giggling slaves who would have kept it filled. He set the scene in his mind against the quiet feast in the long, bare, crowded room in the house of Pudens, with the deep certain voice of Peter falling over them all. He sighed and shifted his position on the silken cushions, turning to answer the drunken confidences of Diomed's father, who sprawled beside him; he knew his own face to be sober with disgust and with his knowledge of the treachery that lay behind the splendor.

As he moved, he caught the eye of Tigellenus. For a brief pause in the gaudy, perfumed clamor they looked at each other with knowledge and directness across the length of the littered tables. And in that bright instant, Justus knew the cold, dark certainty of his own death just as soon as Tigellenus could contrive it. He shifted the golden Falernum, cooled with mountain snow, around the glittering crystal of his cup, and wondered how it would be brought about.

The next day, Nero left the city for his summer villa, swaying in his litter through the hot streets between monstrous feather fans. His thousand baggage wagons filled the narrow roads, and the clacking hooves of the mules that pulled them were shod with silver. On magnificent horses, troops of huge Ethiopians rode before him, their dark faces expressionless above cascades of colored beads, huge silver bangles shifting on their wrists and ankles. As they brushed past his face in the narrow street, a considering merchant put out his hand and fingered their white woolen robes.

"The best!" he whispered to his neighbor. "The very finest Caucasian wool." His face crinkled as he tried to count the cost.

Through the baking city his people watched him go, looking sour and disapproving through the brilliant shoulders of his Guards, and, like the merchant, trying bitterly to count the cost of the train of luxury that followed him. Long enough to still for hours the busy midday streets.

"Hail Caesar!" they dutifully cried, and "Long Live the Emperor!"

Then they turned away to the long hours of toil that must go to pay the taxes that kept him in this gorgeous state, and they murmured and muttered together. Rumor grew that even more was to be pressed from them, for Nero Caesar wanted a new Imperial Palace. He planned it, they said, in gold and marble and lapis lazuli for the mere outside walls. The inside would be of unimaginable costly splendor. All through the hot city, above the carpenter's bench and the rancid vats of the tanner and scorching ovens of the baker, faces were hard and voices resentful when Nero Caesar had passed.

In the hollow of the city, where the river lay like lead under the endless sun, the heat had no effect on the crowds who still gathered daily to hear the words of Peter, and up in the cool, pillared villa of Verius Bautus, the crippled boy could think of nothing else. Despite the scarlet feather fans, the still heat beaded his pale face with sweat, and his restless mind groped endlessly through all he had come to hear of Peter and the Christus who was his Master. He did not even now have the comfort of despair. His mind was torn with the torment of hope. Simon Peter could heal the sick. But there was this confusion that before he could be healed, he must first believe in the Master. He didn't understand.

Since the evening that Gretorix had watched the love feast, both the Praetor Justus Gallius and the lady Pomponia had visited him, talking to him freely of Peter. Justus Gallius looked younger, strangely serene, as though he had made some great decision, and when the lady Pomponia came alone some days later, she sat down beside Diomed and dismissed all the slaves but Gretorix. Her beautiful face shone with happiness under the cloud of her black headscarf.

"The Praetor Justus," she said, "has gone to Anzio with the Emperor, on duty with his Guard. He wishes that I tell you both that he is now baptized. He wanted you, Diomed, especially to know."

The two boys looked at her. Gretorix's face was filled with longing.

"Simon Peter baptized him, my lady?"

"Simon Peter."

"My lady Pomponia." Heat gathered in the room while the scarlet fans were propped against the wall. "My lady Pomponia, surely there is great danger for the Praetor to become a Christian, because of his position. The Emperor likes those about him to think as he does. Is that not true?"

"That is true, Diomed. It is very dangerous—that is why he has been secret about it even with you. At the moment, the Emperor is calm against the Christians, but there is no safety. At least not for those in high places. But," she smiled tranquilly, "the lord Justus has weighed the dangers just as I have myself and knows them nothing to the privilege of entering the Kingdom of God."

Diomed frowned.

"I don't understand about this kingdom, except that the Emperor thinks it threatens the kingdom of Rome."

"It does not. But your mother will question why I stay alone with you so long. I came to bid her goodbye, as she and your father leave for Anzio tomorrow."

"Without me," thrust in Diomed bitterly.

Pomponia did not answer him. She looked over at the young Briton, whose sunburned face had grown gradually to the brown of Rome. "I think your boy Gretorix can soon tell you as much as I can of the Kingdom of God."

"May I speak, my lady?" Gretorix moved from his place at Diomed's head. Pomponia nodded.

"When I watched, my lady, in the house of Pudens, and the scribe of Peter came into the room, he greeted you as the lady Lucina. I have heard much talk these last weeks in the crowds along the river of the lady Lucina, who is the help and hope of all the Christians in Rome. She is endless in her work across the river in the hovels of Transtiberium, helping the poor, nursing the sick, feeding the hungry, caring for the children. My lady, is it you? Lucina, they call her. The Light of Christians. My lady, is it you?"

By the door Pomponia paused, her figure dark against the soft, pale walls, and her face was lit by a great sweetness.

"Many years ago, Gretorix, Peter, our teacher, told me of the words of his Master Himself, when he spoke of these things. Amen, he said, I say unto you, as long as you did it to one of these My least brethren, you did it unto Me."

One night in the still heat of July, when the rumble of the traffic from the distant streets filled Diomed's room in the hot, heavy air, Gretorix came to him with a strange, wide-eyed happiness on his browning face.

Diomed was querulous and irritable in the heat.

"Where have you been? You are gone far longer than I bade you! I have never had you whipped, I have kept you from Mancus and the discipline of the slaves, but that does not mean I always will! Where have you been?"

Gretorix did not answer him, but took the long ivory handle of the fan from Pallius and motioned him from the room. He moved the trembling feathers back and forward above the hot, unhappy boy.

"My lord Diomed, I have been with Peter."

Diomed did not even notice the lack of apology. His ill

temper vanished. The need to know of Peter had grown into an obsession, filling every waking hour.

"Yes."

"My lord Diomed." The fan grew still, and in the soft, shifting light of the oil lamps on the wall, the square, steady face of Gretorix was lit with astonishment and delight. "My lord Diomed. I am a Christian."

He did not look down at the other boy, whose eyes were fixed on him in an agony of misery and frustration.

"I said to you," he went on, "that I wished to go to a love feast of the Christians, but first I must be baptized, and I did not know if I was ready. Today, suddenly, beside the Tiber in all the stench of the sinking river and the pressing crowd, listening to the voice of Peter, I knew the time was come. I could not wait. I thrust my way through the people until I was before him and threw myself at his feet."

There was utter stillness in the room. Gretorix rested the long ivory handle on the floor, and his eyes were wide.

"I begged him to baptize me. He laid a hand upon my head." He paused. "I feel it yet. As though someone laid power itself upon me. And he said, 'Do you believe, my son?' 'Master, I believe,' I said. 'In all I have heard you say and do, I believe.' He answered me—'My son,' he said, 'that is not enough. It is not I.' He lifted up his head and looked about him at the people. A great deep voice he has, and a big, strong face, but strange, mild, unhappy eyes—and he spoke to them all. 'Remember that the Father is in me,' he said. 'The words I have spoken are His words and the deeds I do are His deeds.' It is as I told you, my lord Diomed. And then he baptized me."

Diomed closed his eyes against the exaltation in the other boy's face, fighting desperately against the surge of bitter jealousy that rose to bid him to avenge his own helplessness by treating Gretorix suddenly as he had every right

79

to treat him if he wished—As a slave. To have him beaten for staying out so long, to send him away from being his body slave to some hard, menial task where he would get no time for running after his new God. Anything that would ease the agony of being left out of this thing that shone in the lovely face of Pomponia, that lay serene on the elderly faces of Justus Gallius and Demetrius, and that now lit the excited face of the boy by his side. Of all the miseries of his long illness, never had he been torn by such wretchedness as this. Gradually the tide of hate and anguish receded, and he opened his eyes and looked at Gretorix.

"Gretorix." His voice was hoarse and desperate. "Gretorix. I *must* see Simon Peter, hear his voice, touch him. I must, Gretorix, I must, I must. Half of it all I don't understand, but I am convinced if I could have one finger laid upon the corner of his robe, I would be healed!"

"My lord Diomed!" Gretorix looked on him in pity and despair. "Do you think I have not thought of this? And the lady Lucina? And even my lord Justus? But how, my young lord, are we to get you to him, or he to you? Your parents have gone, but Mancus the Steward is now in charge, and his rule is even more strict than theirs. And he *hates* the Christians. I would have a short life were he to find out about me!"

"There is no real reason why you should not take me in a litter, as Demetrius told me they brought the sick to Jesus when he taught in Galilee. If only I could. I know, oh, I know I would be healed!"

Gretorix's blue eyes were thoughtful, but he had not spoken again when Xania bustled in to remind him resentfully that it was time her young lord slept.

Two mornings later, Gretorix took the ivory handle again from the brown hands of Pallius and sent him from the room. There was little need for the fan. The steady heat was broken by a restless wind blowing from the north,

rustling in the drying trees and whipping the scattered rubbish in the streets to cling round ankles and tangle in the
straps of sandals.

"My lord Diomed." The boy's voice was low and careful,
but thin with a desperate excitement. "My lord Diomed,
tonight the Christians are holding a love feast in one of the
big rooms above the habitations of the dead along the Via
Ostia. The police are growing restless about these gatherings, and they must now be held even more secretly than
before. We could never get a litter from the house unseen,
but you are thin and light, my lord, and I could carry you.
After dark has fallen, Demetrius will help by gathering
the household at some distant point to admire his finished
head, and we can slip out. There is a small gate, little used,
beyond the next court, leading straight upon a lane. I could
hide there the barrow in which your father rides when he
does not want his horse. I could do it, my lord Diomed. I
could do it. And on the Via Ostia will be Simon Peter."

Color came and went across Diomed's face, and his eyes
were mixed in terror and wild hope, but in terror more. It
was one thing to talk of this, but he had seen nothing now
for five years but these painted walls, and the world outside and the thought of the vastness of the nighttime city
filled him with fear. Frantically he searched for an excuse.
Fear drove out all else.

"You could not, Gretorix. You could not carry me."

Gretorix laughed excitedly, looking at the frail, helpless
body he lifted a dozen times a day in order to move it to
ease and comfort, and then looked down at his own strong,
square limbs.

"I could carry you, my lord."

"Well, then." Diomed tried again, panic rising. "How
could we get back in without Demetrius to help us?"

"My lord Diomed." Gretorix walked a little way across
the colored floor and then turned back to look at him.

"Where is your belief in Peter? If we can bring you to his hands, then you will walk back here yourself. And through the great front door."

Diomed grew quiet and lifted his eyes to the sky beyond his windows, where the hot wind sighed and whistled, and the endless blue had changed to the milky haze of storm.

"Yes, of course," he said. "You are right, Gretorix. I will walk home."

In tenseness and anxiety they passed the hours of waiting for the evening darkness, looking at each other secretly when at last the light faded from the squares of the high windows and Mancus and his squad of slaves came in to kindle the lamps along the walls.

"All is well?" Diomed whispered anxiously, as Gretorix helped him with his evening meal.

"All is well. But I must wrap you warmly. There is a strange high wind tonight that is growing cool as darkness falls." He grinned. "Poor good to gain your legs for you and then chill you with a fever."

Diomed tried to grin back, but his teeth were shaking with weakness and anxiety as Gretorix dressed him in a warm woolen robe and for the first time in four long years laced soft boots onto the wasted feet. Sweat lay icy on his forehead as the other boy drew his hood around his face.

"Gretorix, I am afraid."

"Have no fear." Gretorix's square face was bright and confident, hiding the qualms that shook himself. He had not pointed out to Diomed that if the night's work failed, the price to him would be his life.

Demetrius came in with his light, quiet step. He looked at the pale, frightened face of the cripple.

"It is nearly at an end, my son," he said calmly.

"I do not know now, Demetrius, if I am more frightened

that it will succeed or fail!" Diomed tried to still his trembling lips.

Demetrius laid a hand a moment on his head.

"I will go now," he said to Gretorix. "I have placed the head in the atrium, and said that when I come back now to show it, any that are not present will be lacking in respect for the son of their house. They will come, and then shall you go—quickly! And may the blessing of the Christus be upon you both."

The dark colonnades were silent when they crept out, the crippled boy dangling like a sack in Gretorix's strong, young arms. As quickly as he could with his awkward burden, he slipped through the shadows until he faced the small outside door. It was little used, and the bolts were stiff. He cursed himself that he had not thought to oil them. He bent, laid his master on the floor, and tried again, choking with apprehension as the bolts screeched back in their rusted sockets. But there was no other sound, and in a few moments they were outside the house, and Diomed was propped carefully in the cushioned barrow, with the soft, wide, clouded sky above him, and the strange, rising wind whistling past him down the narrow street.

Chapter 7

The high, rich streets of the Esquiline were dark and silent, marked only by the flare of torches above great bronze doors. From far below came the roar and grumble of the nightly traffic, which filled the streets where wheels were not allowed by day, and Gretorix felt a moment's panic at the thought of plunging down into the thick of it. Then he shrugged. They were started now and must go on.

Past the pale, smooth gleam of garden walls he pushed the other boy, filled with a high and desperate excitement.

Many times now he had stood and watched with beating heart and ever-fresh amazement as Simon Peter healed the sick. It seemed only necessary for them to feel the grace of his shadow as he passed. But never had his healing come as close to him as in these hopes for his young master— hopes sharpened with the knowledge that should he be caught in what he did his own most lively hope had best be for a quick and easy death.

He paused a moment as his straining arms grew tired on the steep slope of the hill. He turned the barrow to the side of the road where the ground fell open before them, spattered through the racing clouds with fitful moonlight, and flickering with the shadows of the poplars whose round leaves whispered urgently in the restless wind.

The bright, windy night laid Rome clear below them in all the pale brilliance of her mighty buildings and the crowding darkness of her trees and gardens. They looked over at the marble masses of the Imperial Palace and the sparks of torches crossing and recrossing the wide spaces of the Forum below the rising darkness of the Capitol behind it. Like a marble diadem, the House of Passage crowned the Palatine, looping toward them over the valley in between, which was starred with the lights of Rome. Faintly they could see the shadowy spurs of the nearest hills and the pale, distant gleam of Tiber.

Gretorix gazed over it all and thrust back his long, wind-blown hair. His face was filled with ecstasy in the unstable moonlight. The soft marshes of Britain had given him birth, and at times his heart still grew sick to remember the fall of the dark woods down the green hillsides, and the cool sweetness of a summer dawn when the wild duck rose to his arrows through the flowering reeds. But this was Rome. The Rome of Simon Peter, where he had learned the truth of God. He looked down at Diomed, to share his excitement. Was he not the one who was going to be healed?

But Diomed had closed his eyes and turned away his head from the pale, shadowed city on the seven hills. Terror filled him.

"Take me back, Gretorix!" He could barely speak. "Take me back. I bid you at once!"

It had been too long. For too many years he had lived in the safety of the painted room. Now the world had grown too big for him, and panic struck with the vastness of the night sky and the thought of the crowded streets that lay below, helped by the wind that plucked at his hair and wearied his defenseless face. He no longer wanted to be healed. Gone completely was the urgent, living obsession that he should see the face of Peter and walk away alone from the touch of his hand. All he wanted in this world was to get back to the safety of his pillared room, and the long familiar burden of his helplessness.

"Back, Gretorix!" he cried again. But Gretorix had forgotten that he was a slave. He could only remember that he was a Christian, ecstatic and exalted as were all the Christians of Rome, their senses sharpened by the dangers of their faith. He thought of nothing but to prove this bright faith to his young master. Diomed first ordered and then asked and finally begged and pleaded with tears of fright and weakness on his face. Gretorix only laughed and threw back his hair in the tossing wind, easing his young strength to the barrow on the last steep slopes of the hill.

In the dark, unpaved streets down in the Murcia valley, few people were about. The poor, who lived here in their wooden houses and tottering apartment blocks, kept close at home by night, for there was no money to spend on torches. Those few who crept abroad secretly went as anxious to pass unseen as Gretorix himself. Absently and thankfully, he noticed that no fire watchers seemed to be on duty

86

that night. Round the vast arches of the Circus Maximus, he surprised a group of men gathered in the shadows. One held a torch, lighting the clustered faces and the unlit brands carried by the others. A moment's wonder as to what they could be doing, and he swerved away sharply down a small alley that he knew would take him to the Via Ostia, a narrow street lined with the booths and stores of draperies and clothes, harness and chariot fittings, lamp oil, and all the myriad needs of the great Circus.

Here was pitch darkness, but he knew his way. Diomed was silent now, dumb with terror and bewilderment. Gretorix pressed on blindly over the uneven ground, swerving almost out of control round a corner into a glow of lamplight and a shower of curses from a man who leaped out of his way.

"By the two heads of Janus, boy, where do you think you are going?"

Using all his strength, the boy righted the tilting barrow, and would have rushed on with a muttered apology, laying a hand on Diomed's head to urge him into silence. But Diomed would not be hushed. He was mad with fear.

"Your help, my friend," he cried shrilly. "Your help! I am Diomed, son of Verius Bautus. This is my slave, who is taking me away against my will. He tells some tale that this Simon Peter heals the sick. I don't believe it, and I crave your help to get me back to my home!"

Gretorix's fingers dug into his cheek where he knew that he could feel it, but he would not be silenced, and the Briton cursed him in despair. Here was death, unless he could think quickly.

Before he could do anything, the stranger drew closer, holding up his small, ill-smelling lamp and looking at them both. Behind the circle of light, Gretorix saw his face, swarthy and bearded, with thick, greasy hair curling to his shoulders, and an odd, triumphant smile forming on his thin lips. Strange symbols were embroidered at the neck of his blue robe.

"So," he said, and his voice was not the rough voice that had cursed them when they jumped. Now it was smooth and deep and oddly compelling. "So the young lord goes to be healed by Simon Peter. How foolish!" He laughed gently, and in the darkness Gretorix took a step back. He felt as though evil itself had laid a hand upon his shoulder. "How foolish. Who has told you that this creature can heal the sick?"

Gretorix began to speak, but the man silenced him, bending down to where Diomed's bright, terrified eyes stared up into the lamplight.

"This is nonsense, my young lord, that you have been told. Nonsense. This man can do nothing. He is only a talker. A charlatan."

A short while ago, Diomed had been shouting that he no longer wanted to be healed. Now the terror in his eyes gave way to sick dismay and disappointment. The man smiled —a sleek, professional smile that creased his yellow face but did not touch the dark caverns of his eyes.

"But fate has been good to you, young Diomed," he said. "You have fallen in my path. Or I nearly fell in yours, hm? I can heal you, my son. I have magic far greater than this fellow Peter. I can heal you as I know that he cannot."

"No!" said Gretorix fiercely. He did not know who the man was, but the narrow darkness of the street was filled for him with the certainty of evil, and the yellow face in the small circle of light repelled him with fear and disgust. "No!" he cried again, but Diomed was long past reason, from fear and confusion, and hope given and taken away and given again.

"Yes, yes!" he cried. "I command you, Gretorix. Sir, what do we do?"

The man ignored Gretorix, bending all the time to talk

to the boy in the barrow in his strange, compelling voice.

"Such good fortune for you, my young lord. You are beside a room I have in which I work. You will come with me and find that I have charms to heal you that Simon Peter will never know."

"Simon Peter has the strength of God!"

The man laughed and did not lift his eyes from Diomed. "You will come? You will believe in me?"

"Yes. Yes. I will come. Why should I not believe in you any more than in Peter?" Diomed would believe in anybody who would promise to heal him *now*.

"No!" cried Gretorix again, and moved to seize the barrow, but the man laid a hand upon his arm, and the fingers dug like talons.

"Shall we then call the watch?" he asked.

Gretorix bit his lips in despair. He was not afraid to die, but to be taken now would leave Diomed as he was. Whoever this fellow may be, he was no holy man and would do nothing for him. Again he shivered with the certainty of harm. Better to follow on and try and get them both away.

"All right," he said desperately. "All right." He looked again at the dark face in the small, pale glow of light, smiling now with smooth pleasure. "But who are you, to say that you can heal the sick?"

"Who am I? Your young lord is favored, fellow." In the shadows he drew himself up, and pride was smooth and certain in his voice. "I am Simon Magus. Simon the Magician. There is nothing that is beyond my power."

"Oh!" cried Diomed, and in the small light, foolish hope shone in his face, but Gretorix was silent. Simon the Magician! What wretched ill fortune had brought them to his hands? The meanest slave in Rome knew of Simon Magus, and trembled at his powers, but to all Christians he was known as their unrelenting enemy. Peter was his special target. All round the East he had followed him, striving to undo his work and prove that magic and trickery were more potent than the word of God; he had grown a more bitter and deadly enemy through every year of Peter's patience and indifference. Gretorix had not seen him before; he was newly back from the far south. He nodded now at the boy's silence.

"Exactly, fellow. You may well be silent. Now take your young lord and stay with me."

Frantic but helplessly obedient, Gretorix trundled the barrow along beside the magician, until he paused some way along the street at a low, unlighted door.

"This is *my* place, my secret place," he said with satisfaction as he opened it. "This is not where I see the foolish ladies of the city and tell them empty fortunes for their piles of gold. It is all they deserve! This is where I keep those things that are my own secrets, and here I can cure you, my young lord, as that great loutish preacher never could." His voice was sharp with malice. They were in a small yard, and Simon Magus turned and hung his lantern on a hook, then bent to pick up Diomed from the barrow.

"I will heal you, young master. I will heal you." His voice was soft and insistent and compelling.

Fretting and helpless, Gretorix followed, down a dim passage where small lamps burned on walls of sweating stone, and the soft, monotonous voice murmured hollow over the crippled boy. They circled down a flight of steps where the stone was slippery underfoot with damp, and the air struck dank and icy on their faces in the gloom.

But it was warm in the room at the bottom of the steps, and Gretorix had the feeling that someone left it in the moment they came through the door. The brazier in the middle of the floor was newly banked and threw its rosy glow around the grotesque and horrible objects that crowded every corner of the room. Skulls hung suspended in the air, grinning through their cheekbones in the soft light.

Startled by their coming, a rooster in a vast wicker cage stretched himself on his legs and flapped his helpless wings, crowing as if he felt the dawn. Strange signs were painted on the walls in gaudy colors, and the constellations of the stars crowded above the skulls on the low ceiling. There were books, papers, scrolls, jars, bowls and amphorae, and a basket filled with restless hissing on the floor. Hung from a hook were great swathes of human hair, and tossed idly on a table lay two shriveled hands. Over all was the sense of utter evil which Gretorix had sensed in the man himself when he could barely see him in the dark street. Now he bent to lay Diomed on the couch.

"My lord Diomed," Gretorix cried desperately, and against his voice the rooster crowed again. "Let me take you away. This man is evil!"

Diomed's eyes were roaming wide and frightened now around the horrible room, but he was stubborn. He would not change again.

"No! Let him try! Why should he not heal me just as much as Peter? I have heard of his powers."

Gretorix beat his fists together, and Simon Magus smiled.

"First, my young lord, we must burn away the evil that wastes your limbs. We cannot burn you, but we can burn part of you that is easily come by." Talking steadily all the time in his soft, monotonous voice, he lifted Diomed's limp hands and pared the nails, turning to throw the parings into the brazier. His soft voice lifted in the rhythm of some incantation. Then he reached among the pots and amphorae on the shelves and threw on fistfuls of soft powder that glowed brilliant purple a minute on the coals before it vanished in clouds of pale, aromatic smoke, creeping among the grinning skulls up to the spattered stars, and filling the room with a strange, subtle, and appealing perfume. Gretorix felt his head grow light, and he was filled with a strange content. Simon Magus and Diomed, on the couch, seemed suddenly very far away, and the evil and the danger were foolish things he but imagined. Hazily, through the pale, rising clouds of smoke, he saw the magician pick up a small, close-woven wicker cage and, reaching into it, draw out a fistful of enormous spiders, their great hairy legs waving wildly through his fingers.

"This I have learned from the Egyptians. We will have your legs as free and nimble again, my young lord, as those of these spiders." To Gretorix's swimming head, his voice seemed to boom at him from every side, and then in the next moment to fade into the unimportant distance. "I can do it, young Diomed. I can do it. I place a bowl so above the red-hot coals, and into it I put—"

Gretorix saw the hand reach down to place the spiders in the roasting bowl. He saw rather than heard Diomed cry out, and frantically he shook his fume-filled head and rushed forward. He would die for this night's work in any case, and what harm to add Simon Magus to the deeds that would condemn him? In passing, he seized a statue of the smirking Bast, the dark, evil cat god of the Nile, and leaping past the brazier, he crashed it down on the magician's head.

Diomed was more drugged than he, closer to the fire, and he made no protest as he swept him up. As his staggering run took him out through the door, he looked back, and saw that Simon Magus, as he fell, had taken the brazier with him. He lay beside it on the floor, with him the effigy of Bast, smiling evilly through the white smoke that still rose from the scattered coals.

"Well, if he burns, he burns," thought Gretorix, and stumbled on up the slimy steps, now more desperate than ever to reach Peter and to calm himself under his mild, sad eyes and cleanse himself in the cool, measured words of his preaching from the sense of evil and corruption that crawled under his skin. And to beg him to heal his young master, as only he could do, with the words of God.

Traffic was thick on the Via Ostia, all coming into Rome. The uneven pavings tipped and groaned under the thronging wheels—the farmers with produce for the next day's markets, peasants in small carts with their herbs and honey from the hills, long convoys of the merchants from the port of Ostia with all the produce of the Empire to stack in the warehouses along Tiber banks. The carriages of the wealthy rumbled past the carts of the poor, the chariots of centurions beside the baggage carts of the legions.

The moon was sinking below the hills, and the shadows deepened on the road. Along beside the uproar of the traffic, the houses of the living gradually gave way to the habitations of the dead. Under the dense blackness of tamarisk and cypress, long streets of tombs stretched off on either side—the pagan burial grounds of Rome, where the Christians came in secret to hallow the ground with their own funerals. And in the great chambers above the tombs they gathered under the sign of the fish for the hidden feasts of their faith.

"It's not far now." Gretorix felt his weary arms almost loosing from his shoulders in his efforts to hold his burden steady on the uneven paving and dodge the whips and curses and the ironshod wheels that shaved the sides of the barrow. Only the bright certainty of faith kept him going, and a sick reaction from the evil of Simon Magus made deeper than ever his wondering conviction that, on the way back, Diomed would walk alone.

"I don't care how long it is!" Diomed had recovered now, and his voice was shrill with hysteria. "You had a chance to have me healed and you would not take it!"

"My lord Diomed!" Gretorix was shocked. "That man could never heal you!"

"How do you know? You snatched me away and would not let him try!"

He was utterly confused. He knew only of the distance of black night between him and his familiar room, and that he was helpless himself to return. He had been terrified by Simon Magus, and now he was being taken to some fisherman of Galilee. How was he to know it would not be just the same?

"It is nonsense! Nonsense, all of it. I believe in no one! Take me home!"

Gretorix bent above him and opened his mouth to speak. He never saw the chariot that came behind them, dark horses thundering through the darker night. The driver whirled his three-pronged whip around his head, arrogantly certain that everyone would leave his way.

Gretorix was not hurt—only bruised and shaken, picking himself up from the side of the road and groping in rising panic for the barrow and the other boy. The barrow was broken and the wheels flung wide, and Diomed lay huddled at the foot of a tamarisk, the warm boots sticking out foolishly from the bundle of clothes. Frantically Gretorix called him and shook him. In the name of all I believe, he thought foolishly, Peter can heal the sick, but unless he can raise the dead, then I am dead myself. He calmed himself and felt the young Roman's temple, then blew out a long, whistling breath. He must have hit the tree and stunned himself. He could yet reach Peter.

Long later, Gretorix stumbled up the stone stairs on the outside of a huge family tomb. He was dazed and confused by his fall, weary from the struggles of the night, yet he still carried the other boy in his aching arms, blind to everything except the need to get to Peter. His young lord may have lost his courage, and fear had stolen his faith, but it might be that his own faith would serve for two of them. On the wide stone steps, he paused a moment to sniff

94

stupidly at some strange, acrid tang that touched the moaning wind, and to look back dazedly at a faint, rosy haze that seemed to hang above the distant city. He shook his tired head and plodded on upward.

The long room was packed, silent under the deep, quiet voice of Peter, who preached from a chair at the far end of it; his deacons gathered round him, and Mark, his scribe, sat at his feet. Gretorix could see him from the door, slightly above the people, holding them fast in the fall of his strong, even voice, his great gray head bent to them in loving admonition. He felt a great calm. It was only necessary now to reach that quiet figure in the chair and all would be well.

"Gretorix!" A hand seized him from behind, and a voice sharp with amazement asked him what he did. He struggled round, and Justus Gallius gazed down astonished at the unconscious Diomed. "What are you doing? His parents cannot know of this. I left them in Anzio."

Under his plain, dark cloak, Gretorix could see the golden glint of the Praetor's armor. The lord Justus also should be at Anzio with his Divine Majesty. We are truants both, he thought, and gladly allowed Justus to take the limp body of the boy from his arms.

"I would have him healed," he said. "I brought him secretly, and to begin with he had the faith to come." Weariness overwhelmed him, and despair that it was all in vain. "But now I do not know. Is my faith enough for him?" His fair young face was white with exhaustion, and the older man looked at him, and his reproaches died before he spoke them.

"Let us wait," he said gently, "until Peter is done preaching and the people move. Then we can get near, my son, and see if the faith of two of us will be enough for three."

Gretorix blinked. He is my friend, he thought, and not only my master. I a slave from the edges of the world, and he a Praetor of Rome, yet since we are both Christians there is no difference between us. The warmth and love of his new faith flowed over him like a tide, and he turned then to listen to the steady voice that preached of all he had come to believe. But Peter was finished. As Gretorix turned to listen, he stood up, towering at the far end of the room above all those around him; his face was lined with the sadness that never left it. He raised his hand and blessed the people, and there was silence in the hot, crowded room. Then they stirred and sighed, as though a wind had passed across them where they stood.

Diomed was coming back to consciousness, swimming into memory of the dark, terrifying journey and the wild hopes roused by the magician. He was dimly aware of a bare, white ceiling above his head, the massed people that jammed about him, and a strong, quiet voice that spoke like the voice of a god from some unfathomable distance.

In the silence after the voice had stopped, there was the sound of running feet and the crashing open of a door; then another voice yelled in fright and urgency that the city was on fire. Rome was burning at half a dozen places, and all must come at once to try to save their homes and children. He sensed the gasping and dismay, and the rising murmur of alarm and the frantic crushing of the crowd toward the door. He was lying on some sort of couch, and he could not see Gretorix. Tears of fear rose in his exhausted eyes that, in the rush and panic, he had been forgotten.

Then in the center of the uproar came a calm, and a quiet face that bent close above him with tendrils of gray hair around a balding head, and the saddest dark-brown eyes that he had ever seen.

"He is not yet ready," said the voice which he had thought of as the voice of a god, and then the face was gone. And so were the people. His mind cleared, and he saw that he was alone with Justus Gallius and his British slave. They stood beside him in some vast, strange, bare room, and there were tears hot on his face for some nameless sadness, and a sense of loss greater than any grief he had ever dreamed.

Chapter 8

In silence the two beside him looked at each other, and Justus laid a hand on Gretorix's shoulder.

"It is not enough." He smiled sadly. "It is not enough, for two to have faith for three. We must all have faith. Patience, Gretorix, my son. Patience. Now, unless this is to lead to death, we must get you back, and no one must ever know. The city is on fire, they say, and I should be in Anzio. But come—I can take the boy before me on my horse, and you can run with me."

Justus picked up the boy. When they got outside, the sky above the city trembled with a flickering, scarlet glare, and the strengthening wind was sharp and acrid with the smell of fire. Gretorix gazed at it in sick, lurching fright as he remembered the magician lying on the floor beside the spilled coals and the smiling face of Bast.

"This is no small fire," said Justus. "It seems to be in many places." And Gretorix licked his dry lips and felt his stomach settle. He ran down the steps behind Justus, who had the speechless Diomed in his arms.

"Quickly, boy! I must be back at Anzio before this news reaches the Emperor. Quickly!"

Somehow they propped the helpless boy before him on the horse, and with Gretorix running at the stirrup, they turned their faces to the burning city. Much of the wheeled traffic going into Rome had come to a halt. Carts stood beside the road, and fearful drivers clustered together and stared across the distance at the trembling glow that grew every moment wider across the dark hills. Near the Ostian Gate, the traffic was already beginning to pour the other way; there were processions of carts and barrows laden with families and household goods. Hurrying, thickening crowds of wide-eyed people, shrill with alarm, fled with their weeping children in their arms from their burning homes to the wide, safe spaces of the Campagna. Justus did not pause to question them, cursing softly as they slowed the pace of his horse, and through the panic stricken rush inside the gate, Gretorix had to cling tightly to his stirrup leather, struggling not to be swept away. He coughed and gasped for breath against the falling ash that now filled the hot wind, and threw anxious glances at Diomed, held tight in the arm of Justus, his shocked eyes wide on the red glare toward which they rode.

The Circus Maximus was burning furiously, the scarlet flames licking across the narrow streets to grasp at the shops and booths and roar suddenly into fresh life, fanned into fury by the wind. In the Circus itself the stables were ablaze, and small figures darted dark against the sheets of flame, trying hopelessly to reach the horses through the roaring fire and the crash and rumble of collapsing masonry.

Before they realized it, almost as if it came to meet them like a living thing, Justus and Gretorix were in the heart of the fire. The small streets were lit like scarlet day and full of shouting people running here and there in terror and distraction, some trying to help, some trying to get away, some simply running, their hair singed and the flames still licking round the edges of their clothes, mad with grief for the houses that had crashed behind them and the families they had lost.

Justus had trouble with the horse, dancing with terror and threatening to fling Diomed from his one-handed grasp.

"Upward!" he yelled at Gretorix, coughing in the effort to speak. "Upward. There is no fire higher up!"

Gretorix did not see how he knew. Down here in the Murcia valley, the whole world was filled with fire. Even as it terrified, it reassured him. In so short a time, the one small fallen brazier in the deep cellar of Simon Magus could never have grown to so great a fire. Relief was sweet in his parched throat.

"Here, my lord, soon," he gasped back to Justus. "A little road that turns up to Coelius. Very soon."

He prayed frantically to his newfound God. Every moment brought fresh fountains of flame, and ahead of them the buildings crumbled black into their own blazing ruins and down in burning piles into the roadway. He looked back in time to see a tall apartment house topple, breaking like the castle of a child down onto the small, dark figures that darted frantically from beneath it. There was no going back.

The small road was an avenue of flame when they reached it. Gretorix dragged his breath into his hot, tearing lungs and looked at Justus. The soldier's face was calm in the dancing glare, and the boy felt himself grow calmer too. Diomed was wrapped completely in his cloak and hood, long past knowing of his danger. Across the road ahead of them another building crashed, and Justus in turn looked down at the boy.

"We have no choice, my son," he shouted, and his voice was almost gone. He strained, one-handed, at the terrified horse. "And less choice if we are slow."

In the narrow space of the street within the roaring circle of the flames, he looked down at Diomed and then at Gretorix. Red fire danced and glinted in the golden leaves of his Praetorian armor, and lit the purple stripe of rank along his tunic. His cracked lips smiled slightly at the slave.

"Our Christus be with us," he said, and they plunged into the cave of flame.

Gretorix had little memory of how he got out. He remembered only the heat, the scorching heat that struck at his eyeballs and seared his throat, so that he put his head down and ran blindly, clinging to the leaping horse and holding his free hand hopelessly above his head to protect him from the burning fragments that blew like hot rain in the wind. He did not see the building fall. He heard the hoarse, desperate shout of Justus above him, and felt the horse fling itself forward. The roaring crash was just behind them, but some loose flying fragment took Justus on his uncovered head and knocked him from the saddle. Neighing like a lost devil, the horse was gone, thundering through the avenue of fire. Justus lay unconscious on the ground, and for the second time in that monstrous night, Gretorix searched frantically for Diomed.

He could not take them both. Desperately he paused

a moment, and then picked up the boy, flung clear as Justus fell. He looked at the sprawled body of the soldier and blindly shook his head, struggling with the quick thoughts that sprang up even in this terrible moment in the red, flaming street of terror—thoughts of the long distant days when he had lost his mother and his father and his home, and this strange, important Roman had taken him, and helped to heal his loss with gentleness and thought.

"I am sorry, my lord Justus," he said hoarsely, and the tears were agony on his scorched eyeballs. "I am sorry."

Then he turned and ran as fast as fear could take him up the burning street.

It was like another world when at last he laid his burden down in the same sheltered spot where only hours before he had paused to allow Diomed to look at Rome. He was well above the fire. Even here, the wind was hot and filled with ash, but he could breathe it deep and desperate into his scorched lungs. For the moment he did not dare to look at Diomed.

The fire was in a great ring all round the Circus Maximus, and crept already up the Palatine, glowing like a frenzied dawn behind the splendid arches of the House of Passage. It must have started in half a dozen places at least, the boy thought dumbly. It must have *been* started, to have got so far, so soon. He shook his head. Who would want to burn Rome? He almost laughed now at his own sick fear that he had started it himself with his handful of coals in the magician's cellar.

There was no time to think about it now. If he wished to live to see this fire burn out, he must find some way of getting his young lord safely back without being seen. Though how the boy would be . . . He turned then to Diomed on the grass beside him, his wide, astonished eyes fixed on the burning city down below. He did not look as if he saw.

"My lord Diomed," he said to him. "Are you all right?"

Diomed turned his eyes to him. Even up here they could see each other clearly in the dancing glow, and he looked at the slave's blackened face and the singed ends of his long hair.

"I have left my chamber tonight for the first time in five long years," he said, and his voice was faint and hoarse. "I have seen Peter face to face, and seen you and my lord Justus near to death for me, and now I watch Rome burning here below me." The thin voice grew slower, and Gretorix thought with a pang of wretchedness that he did not realize that Justus had come more than near to death. "All these things," Diomed went on faintly, "and they are nothing. I am not walking back."

Diomed blinked his singed eyelids and held to his patience.

"You are lucky, my lad," he almost said, "to be getting back at all. You are not yet back, and my lord Justus lies where we have left him. There will be people out all over the hilltops to watch the fire. You do not walk tonight— I will be lucky if I am alive to walk tomorrow!"

But he did not say it. He bent and picked the boy up again, wincing at the weight on his scorched arms.

"There is time, my young lord. Peter did not say no. He only said you were not ready. I have done my best tonight, and I beg you do not betray me now as I try to get you home."

Diomed did not answer him, and Gretorix could not read the expression in his eyes. He crept along the shadows of the walls, listening to excited voices on the terraces above his head, and dodging away from the chattering, excited groups gathered at the vantage points that overlooked the city. Once or twice he could not avoid the frantic questions of someone anxious for a lost relative down in the blazing valleys, but he was never questioned for himself, and Diomed was accepted as a victim from the flames. Nor did he speak to contradict.

Gretorix was below the garden walls of the Villa Verius, his tired mind still frantic for a way of getting back into the house. He paused in the deep shadow of a clump of olives and turned his face away from the ceaseless wind that nagged his burns.

"My lord Diomed," he said desperately. "I do not know what to do. If I am caught now, I will die."

Diomed looked at him with empty eyes.

"I was not healed," was all he said.

Gretorix looked at him in exasperation, tempted for the first time to abandon him and run. Patience ran low, fear gripped him, and he was very tired. With an effort he remembered that this night's work was his idea, and the boy was sick. The events of these last hours had been enough to throw the balance of the strongest. A hand laid on his shoulder from behind made him so leap with fright he all but dropped his master.

"Demetrius," he said weakly, and hardly knew if he would laugh or weep. "Demetrius. I thought it was the watch! Or Mancus the Steward! Oh, Demetrius, what am I to do? I can't get back into the house!"

"I was waiting for you, lest this might happen. Give him to me awhile." He smiled to calm the exhausted, panic-stricken face, and took Diomed from his arms. "I don't know what has happened down there tonight." He nodded at the city. "But what went wrong with you? And with the young lord?"

Gretorix shrugged.

"Peter said he was not ready. Demetrius, *how shall I get in!*"

"Ah." The Greek was calm. "There is time yet."

"So my lord Justus said. *Demetrius—*"

"Justus Gallius?" Now the voice was sharp, edged with anxiety.

"Yes, yes. He was there tonight on the Via Ostia. He brought us back into the city, and hoped to bring us home."

"And now?"

"Demetrius, I could not help it." Gretorix had forgotten his own danger, and his blackened face crumpled in grief. "I could not help it! A building fell and he was hit. He was senseless. I had to leave him. I couldn't take them both. Could I? Could I?" His singed eyelids blinked away tears of weariness and loss.

The Greek's face was calm and reassuring.

"He may yet escape. But that could be worse for him. Nero will ride from Anzio at this news, and he will need a Guard, and the Guard a leader. Tigellenus will not fail to notice who is missing. But that is tomorrow's trouble. Now, listen carefully. The whole household stands up on the terrace, watching the fire, but that is not enough. They may leave it. I will give them something to keep them closer occupied. Wait here. When you see smoke rising from the stables, then go in quickly, through the door you came out."

"Smoke?" Had there not been enough smoke for one night?

"Yes." Demetrius smiled grimly in the shadows, and the wind blew his hair into a wild halo round his head. He looked down at the city and the cloud that grew redder and more dense with every hour. "Fire! That is the one cry that will bring everybody running tonight!"

The stable yard was deserted, all the slaves having gathered, chattering and speculating, on the terraces that overlooked the city. In a safe corner, distant from the horses, Demetrius made a pile of straw and unhooked the oil lamp from the wall. No one knew who shouted "Fire!" or who was the first to smell the burning from the stables, but, as the Greek had foreseen, the whole overexcited household raced shouting to the cry. And the small, quiet courts at the back of the house were empty. Xania alone might have thought of Diomed, and she was at Anzio with her mistress.

In the shadows beyond the stables Demetrius listened with satisfaction to the noise inside and slipped away. Through the red glow of the night, Mancus the Steward walked back along the hillside from where he had climbed to get a better view of the fire. He saw smoke rising from his master's villa and broke into a run, throwing only a brief, sharp glance at the shadowy figure who stood close into the wall as he passed.

Diomed was little scorched, for Justus had protected him well with the covering of the cloak. When Gretorix had laid him at last safely in his own bed, he turned and bolted the big doors of the chamber, and leaned on them for one long moment of sick relief. Then he set frantically to work, cutting off the singed fragments from the dark hair and dressing the boy's few burns with colored ointment. He could say his master had caught some rash. With Xania away, there would be no one to question him too much. At last he stood back and looked at Diomed, still wide-eyed and silent, and wiped his sore hands in satisfaction on the front of his tunic. Safe and clean again under his fringed, embroidered counterpane, no one would ever know he had been out. Gretorix gave a giggle of light-headed pleasure. His master's hair looked a little rough! He could blame the barber. Then his face sobered and his hands grew still, arrested by the expression in the eyes of Diomed.

"There is still time, my young lord," he said gently, as he had said before. The thin face did not change, nor did he answer, and Gretorix shrugged. For the moment, let it be. For him, just now, it was enough to be alive. He picked up a mirror and looked at his own almost lashless eyes, his singed and blistered skin, and the brittle, burned ends of his long hair. It would be useless to say he had not been out that night. The fire had laid its mark on him, and it had started long after he had any right to be abroad. Diomed was in no state to save him. Wryly he squared his sore shoulders to face the inevitable beating from Mancus.

Chapter 9

At Anzio the Emperor had been fishing, trawling in the dark green seas beyond the rocks with a golden net, floated by bright bubbles of blown and gilded glass. He was at the landing stage when the courier came from Rome, stumbling down the marble staircase from the terrace into the green, shifting shadows and the salt smell of nets and fresh-caught fish.

"Hail Caesar!" he cried, and his face was blanched with the speed of his journey and the terror of the news he bore. "Mighty Caesar!" He had to put a hand on the ground to steady himself on one knee. "Mighty Caesar! Rome is on fire! The city burns from end to end!"

Nero looked at him and did not speak. He turned and went slowly up the shadowy staircase into the full sun on the terrace above, to stand with his hands on the marble wall, gazing in the direction of his city of Rome. There was nothing to be seen above the hills that lay between, and around him his Court made light of the story. Was not Rome always burning somewhere? There was no city in the Empire more desperately in need of rebuilding down in the poor quarters. They shrugged. It would be as it always was. The firemen would hold the fire into an "island," and that would be the end of it. They urged Nero to think nothing of it and pursue his holiday.

"Forget it, Caesar," urged Tigellenus, lounging at his side. "Is not the city always somewhere on fire? It will make but another open space that your Majesty can plant with new gardens for the beauty of Rome."

Nero's pale eyes slid round to him, and they were cold as amber from the dark countries of the north.

"A garden? In place of the houses of my people? I who am the Father of Rome?"

Tigellenus drew back. He had struck the wrong note, miscalculated the mood of his incalculable master, and Nero's considering eyes stayed on the distant hills. By dusk they were crowned with a red, trembling glow and the unstable shadows of far-off smoke, whipped by a ceaseless wind. With every hour, fresh, panting couriers brought messages of terror. The Circus was engulfed, fed by the shops and booths all round it, filled with oil and wax and clothes to help the flames. The fire was beginning to creep up the hills, and from whole burning districts the people were pouring screaming from the city. The gods had spoken and Rome was at an end. How did it start? The messengers did not know. They only knew it had started in eight different places at the same time.

Tigellenus summoned the Tribune of the Guard.

"Have the Guard stand ready," he ordered. "The Emperor will leave shortly for the city. The Praetor Justus Gallius will ride with you."

The Tribune looked uncomfortable, easing from one leather-booted foot to the other.

"The Praetor is not in his quarters, sir. Nor in ours," he said uneasily. "He has not been seen since he rode out last night toward Rome. He was in uniform, but rode bareheaded. He rode alone."

Tigellenus lifted his eyebrows, and his narrow eyes slid in pleased speculation toward the city. Had fortune given him two birds with one stone from the sling? He turned back to the Tribune.

"I see," he said smoothly. "Well, then, you will take command in his stead."

"Sir." The Tribune looked at him doubtfully. He hoped he had done no harm to the Praetor Justus Gallius, who was worth twenty of this sly-eyed worm. But if he did not speak now, at the next count his own neck might be under the ax. He shrugged as he walked away in the creak of leather and the click of nailed boots. A soldier as old as the Praetor should be well able to look after himself.

The Emperor rode all through the night toward his city. Tigellenus was at his side, his weasel face inscrutable, and behind him jingled the small brilliant company of Guards who should have been the charge of Justus Gallius. In the last dark before the dawn, they drew their horses on the crest of the Alban Hills and took their first clear look at the city.

"The space that this will clear, Tigellenus my friend, will make a handsome garden." Nero's voice was appalled and sarcastic when at last he spoke, his horrified eyes fixed on the sea of red and yellow mist that writhed over the tops of the seven hills, patched with the torn, dark clouds of drifting smoke. Already they met the people in terrified flight, unwilling to pause even to answer their questions, for once utterly indifferent to the face of their Emperor and the gold and scarlet glory of his Guard. All who did pause to answer said the same thing. The fire had started in several places at once, but all of them somewhere round the circle of the Circus Maximus.

Dawn came as they crossed the Campagna. The hollows of the soft, rolling grass were still filled with mist, and the larks flung themselves into the lightening sky, indifferent to the swarms of anguished people spreading frantically over the open spaces in search of safety.

They were into the city through the Porta Capena before Nero heard the first murmurs.

"Do not concern yourself!" one man shouted to another as they jostled against his horse. "It is the Emperor who orders this! He has to burn the city to burn his palace, that he may build a new one!"

"Yes—but will he rebuild my house?"

Unaware and indifferent, they shouted across the Emperor's startled face.

Staggered, Nero looked across at Tigellenus, whose narrow face was utterly without expression. He pulled his cloak close over his head and pressed on to the Imperial Palace. It was not destroyed. The flames had not yet reached up the Quirinal, but the servants had all fled, terrified at being surrounded on their hill by the furiously blazing district below them in the valley.

Three nights and days the fire raged in the center of Rome, defying all the efforts of the fire brigades and salvage men to get it out. As fast as they closed it safely in an "island," and thought themselves at last successful, the flames rose again somewhere outside their cordon. But on the fourth day they succeeded, and the flames were dead. Dark smoke hung like a pall above the city, and the air was still full of the rumble of collapsing buildings and choked with the smell of fire and the foul, mumbling dryness of falling ash. But the flames were dead. In wonderment and thanksgiving the demented people turned to gaze at each other with hope growing in their eyes. Perhaps the damage may not be so immense after all. They breathed again and began to creep back timidly to pick with hopeless fingers among the charred and smoking ruins of their homes.

By nightfall the flames were leaping once again, tall as the statue of Jupiter himself on the great temple on the Capitol. The city was wild with fear and screaming with alarm.

"It is the bidding of the Emperor!"

"It started afresh in the gardens of his best friend, Tigellenus!"

"Nero Caesar orders that Rome burns!"

It was no avail that through the terror-stricken days and nights that followed, Nero himself struggled through the narrow lanes of Rome, his face blackened, his tunic burned, and his red curls singeing in the heat, offering help wherever he might. More often than not, in their terror, his people did not know him, and if they did, he was reviled.

Stricken with grief to see his city destroyed and his people reject him, he stood on the fifth evening on the terrace of the Palace, watching the flames that crept up remorselessly toward the lower end of his gardens. Tigellenus moved out beside him, a lyre in his hand.

"It is a sad, sad sight, Majestic Caesar. Never, I think, has there been such a subject for a tragic lyric. Never such a subject for your divine gifts of composition, and your matchless voice. Take your lyre, Caesar. Take your lyre and sing for us the immortal dirge of burning Rome."

Ever gratified by the dramatic moment, Nero looked at Tigellenus and his dull eyes grew bright. He seized the lyre and looked down across the blazing slopes through the drifting smoke. He would inspire his people with his song, let them know the depths to which their plight moved him. His fingers wandered on the strings and his face grew rapt. Lifting up his head, he threw his golden voice with all his strength out across the cauldron of heat and death. He could scarcely hear it himself, drowned in the endless hiss and roar and rumble of the fire. Disconsolate, he threw down the lyre and turned away. But in these few moments, high upon the terrace, he had been seen.

In the crowded districts at the bottom of the hill, the people ran shouting through the burned-out streets.

"He cares so little that, even as we burn, he sings up on his terrace!"

"The Emperor rejoices while Rome burns!"

"Nero sings!"

Hate poured then like the fire itself up toward the Palace, and Tigellenus, sensing it, smiled behind his hand and congratulated himself on the success of all his plans. It should not be long now. His only doubt and disappointment lay in the disappearance of Justus Gallius, but he was reassured when, on the seventh day, he saw him back. He was inspecting the Praetorian Guard drawn up around the Palace with their lances couched, ready to repel attack from the hordes of ownerless slaves who killed and pillaged through the stricken city. Tigellenus looked at him, and Justus Gallius looked evenly back. His uniform was immaculate again, but the burns were still raw on his hands and face, and an unhealed wound ran along one temple under the rim of his gilded helmet.

"I am glad to see you back, Justus," his commander said smoothly. "We have missed you."

And for some reason, thought Justus, it suits your book

not to tell the Emperor and have him miss me also. What is your plot now?

"This, I take it, sir," he said, and lifted a hand to the charred and smoldering streets, "is the evil that you hope to lay at Caesar's door, to get Rome to remove him from the throne. Clever, Tigellenus, clever! But do not underestimate your Emperor. You have not pinned the blame to him yet. I should wait a little to put on the Imperial cloak."

He turned and walked away, and the face of the other man was ugly as he watched.

"My proud Justus!" he said to himself. "If I do not succeed in pinning the blame to the Emperor, then I will pin it somewhere else that will give me almost equal satisfaction."

By the end of the seventh day the fire was over, halted by a vast firebreak across the foot of the Esquiline. Two thirds of the city, below its pall of smoke, lay in blackened ruins. In the temples and on all the open spaces the homeless people camped, without food or clothes, muttering openly against their Emperor, and roaming the desolated city in angry bands to loot and steal. Among the homeless crowds, strange stories ran, as the fire had run through the huddled streets. Just before it started, dark figures had been seen lurking round the Circus Maximus with torches in their hands. People whispered of sudden bursts of flame where sparks could never blow. All the fire watchers had been mysteriously off duty. Soldiers sent to quell the fire had been seen to spread it with fresh brands. In the roving, frantic crowds among the smoking ruins, talk ran wild and resentment piled against Nero Caesar, who had burned Rome for his own ends. Had he not, they cried in despair, given proof of his indifference, that in the middle of the agony of his city, he had climbed the terrace of his palace to sing above the flames?

As soon as he could safely do it, Justus Gallius turned his horse upward through the firebreak on the Esquiline to where the quiet streets on the hilltop lay undisturbed, and the white walls of the Villa Verius were only faintly blackened by the days of rising smoke. Mancus the Steward was still in charge, bowing before him by the fountain in the atrium.

"No, my lord Praetor," he said in answer to his question. "My lord Bautus and the lady Gallia did not come back from Anzio. They sent message that they heard we were well above the fire, and they saw no need."

Justus' face tightened.

"And the young lord Diomed?" he asked as casually as he could, his throat tight with anxiety for the two boys.

Mancus made a gesture of irritation.

"The young lord has a fever," he said shortly, without sympathy, as if annoyed that Diomed should so trouble his stewardship. "I have called in the physicians and they find no cause for it. The cause I see is that his British slave neglects him. Out in the city when he should be watching over his master!" His face was grim with satisfaction. "It will be long before he goes down into the city again at night. He got double punishment—a burning from the fire and a beating from me!"

Justus raised indifferent eyebrows, and winced as the movement caught the gash across his temple.

"The slave was burned in the fire?"

Mancus laughed. "That was why I knew he had been out. His skin was all scorched, and the room full of the smell of burning hair. You are wounded yourself, my lord, and burned, I see. But you, no doubt, were in the fire in the line of duty."

Justus ignored his obsequiousness, and his calm, brown face hid the tide of relief that somehow the two boys had got back and both were safe.

115

"I will see the young lord awhile," he said.

Mancus shrugged.

"He will not know you, my lord." His voice was indifferent.

"I will see him nevertheless." Justus looked at him and Mancus bowed at once, clasping his hands over the leather bracelets on his wrists before he clapped for a slave to lead the Praetor to the boy.

At the door of Diomed's room, he brought all the authority of his military life to bear in a long steady stare at Gretorix; and he, after one wild, startled glance, understood what his lord required. Carefully he stood up from where he knelt beside the bed, and bowed, showing no surprise that Justus should be there. Fuscus the Dumb was putting in his hopeless hours of massage on the helpless legs, and Gretorix turned and bade him go, along with the boys who waited on him to carry his ointments and his towels, and also Pallius, on duty with his feather fan. His fair face was immobile, and he did not look at Justus through the long minutes while the room emptied.

Only when the bronze door closed did he come down the steps at a great leap, forgetting slavery, forgetting the penalty of death for laying an uninvited slave's hand on a citizen of Rome.

"My lord Justus! My lord!" In his voice was all the tight anxiety and grief of these past days when he had thought him dead. "I *had* to leave you! I could not take you and my young lord! I would not willfully have left you. I thank the Christus you are safe. I have *prayed!*"

"Peace, Gretorix! Peace." He looked kindly down on the anxious face and loosed the anxious hands. "I am all right, but take my helmet. It is sore on a sore head." He winced as he lifted off the weight of gilded silver pressing painfully, even with its padded lining, on the open wound. The burned patches were still raw in his gray hair. "That is better." Gretorix laid the purple plumes beside him on the floor, and Justus turned to the boy who lay in the bed, the uneasy, noisy breathing of his fever loud in the quiet room. "You got him back."

"Yes, my lord Justus. It was Demetrius." Quickly he told the soldier how the Greek had helped them back, and Justus nodded.

"God was with you. But all is not well with your young master now."

Gretorix walked up and looked sadly at Diomed, at the hot, unhappy face and the dark, fevered eyes that roamed the shadows of the ceiling and saw nothing at all.

"It was too much for him, my lord—the fear of the journey." He paused. No need to tell the Praetor of the added danger they had faced in the cellar of Simon Magus. "The fire. But most of all, I think, to know that in the end he was not healed."

"He was not ready."

"Fear had lost him his faith. How did Peter know that, even though my young lord could not speak?"

Justus' eyes were quiet on his face.

"Peter would know, my son, whether he could speak or not. I have been with him these last days, down in that inferno in the city."

"With Peter?"

"Yes. I was lucky when you had to leave me. I fell between two houses built of stone. I was almost scorched to death, but they didn't fall on me. When I was conscious again, I wandered dazed through the streets, scarce able to remember who I was. There were people trapped in burning houses, screaming and clamoring for help in tumbled ruins. I forgot Nero Caesar and I forgot his Guard, and turned to help. Down in the Suburra, where the houses are thickest and the fire swept the streets like wind, I fell among the Christians."

Gretorix waited for him to go on. And after a moment, Justus raised his head, and his tired, scorched, elderly face was soft with reverend affection.

"Peter was everywhere," he said. "Everywhere. Where the fire was thickest and the danger greatest, plunging into burning houses and staggering out with great armfuls of children held against his chest. I saw him once with his hair on fire, like a crown about his head. He was everywhere—comforting the homeless, calming the frenzied, giving peace to the dying. And many more with him, doing all they could to help."

His face darkened when he stopped, and again the boy waited for him to go on.

"But there were others," he said heavily, "who marched through the blazing streets, rejoicing in the old prophecies that foretold the burning of the city, laughing and dancing as the flames ate up the houses, and refusing help to the trapped and helpless. They rejoiced, they screamed, in the death of every Roman, as it made way for the Kingdom of God!"

Gretorix shook his head slowly, appalled and unable to understand these Christians who so forgot the love that Peter preached, and confused the Kingdom of God with the Kingdom of Rome. But he still did not understand the desperate gravity of the Praetor's face, or why he sat so still, his eyes on the mosaics between his feet, with this strange look of resigned sadness.

"What is it, my lord?" he asked.

The older man looked at him reflectively and then at the delirious boy beside him.

"It is nothing," he said. "Nothing that will trouble you. You care for your young lord, and try to ease his fever. Leave the city to itself."

He stood up, easing himself stiffly from his chair as

though he had suddenly grown old. Gretorix bent for his helmet, and the purple plumes ruffled with his breath.

"Mancus the Steward is a Jew, is he not?" Justus asked casually.

"Yes." Gretorix was puzzled. "He was, my lord Diomed told me, in the household of the lady Poppaea, who is of the Jewish blood and likes her servants to be so. She sold him to the lady Gallia when her old Steward died. This is why he so hates the Christians, being of the Jewish faith, and also from the royal house. Why, my lord?" he added diffidently, too curious to hold his tongue.

Justus paused before the great double doors, and looked again at the two boys.

"He knew," he asked, not answering the question, "that you were out on the night of the fire?"

"My lord Justus, I could not help it. You know how burned I was, my hair singed off in great pieces. I hid my young lord's burns, but I could not hide my own. Why, my lord, why?"

Gretorix was anxious and worried, touched with a fear he did not understand. Justus turned on him the firm, authoritative look that had steadied long years of fearful young soldiers when the trumpets blew the charge.

"Nothing, Gretorix. Nothing at all. Care for your young master. Now call the housemen to show me out."

As Gretorix flung open the bronze door, he struck someone just outside. Mancus jumped aside and at once collected himself. With a baleful glance at the British boy, he bowed to Justus.

"I was just coming in," he said, "to offer the lord Praetor some refreshment."

Chapter 10

Nero was frantic to regain the confidence of his people before the fire swept him from the Imperial throne as it had swept the buildings from the streets of Rome. He threw open all his private gardens to house the homeless and threw open the Treasury to provide them with food and clothes. And the people took his money and built their tents among the flowers around his marble fountains, then watched in doubt and indifference when he led vast processions to the Temples of Ceres and Proserpine and Jupiter, offering sacrifices to appease the anger of the gods who had cast down fire on Rome. They were not convinced.

Anxiously he watched their silent faces in the ruined streets, and his mind was haunted by the voices that had shouted across his horse above the crackle of the flames that he had burned Rome above their heads for his own pleasure, and for the building of a new Palace. By the third week, he laid in triumph before the Senate his plans for a new Rome. He would show his muttering people that Nero Caesar lived only for them. From all corners of the Empire, men and materials were commanded to be rushed to the capital. The ships that daily crept up Tiber with food for the hungry people went back down again to the marshes by the sea, piled with the debris of the ruins that were clearing like summer snow under the hands of an army of workmen.

He planned for them treelined streets and big, well-proportioned houses, new rows of shops and palatial public buildings, large apartment blocks with private courts and fountains, all of them solidly built of stone and concrete, that the terror of fire might never strike again. The city rang with the frenzy of building—the thud of mallets upon paving stones, the clang of hammers, the rasp of saws, and the voices of workmen from all corners of the Roman world. The fine stone houses began to rise like magic along the widened streets, and the citizens watched in delight and disbelief. Along the freshly planted avenues, Nero stepped in his new, fashionable, thick-soled sandals, gathering his toga close around him against the dust of building, and nodding his red curls in satisfaction. He began to smile again, having bought back the approval of his people, and behind him the smooth expectant face of Tigellenus crumbled into growing doubt.

Then he lost his head. From the smoke-blackened terraces of the Imperial Palace, across his burned-out gardens, he looked daily over at the tragic ruins of Caligula's House of Passage, in whose splendid colonnades treasures of uncounted value had perished in the fire. The once-glorious springing arches now crumbled over the blackened hillside across the valley like a row of broken teeth. It was the finest site in the whole city, and for the Emperor the temptation was too much. While the new houses of his people were only half-risen in the valleys, Nero took the Palatine Hill and all the slopes of land around it. He demolished the ragged teeth of the broken arches of the House of Passage, and on the summit of the hill began the building of his new Palace.

Money was taken from everything else. The architects and builders were offered all the resources of the Empire and every last coffer in the Treasury to produce a building worthy of their Emperor. Workmen were withdrawn in thousands from the rising streets of Rome, and in seven short months, the Palatine was crowned with the vast, glittering walls of Nero's Golden House, the most costly Palace Rome had ever seen. Down in the city, the hungry and homeless people stood among the half-built, abandoned houses and stared up at it in silence.

"I wish I could find words to tell you of it, my lord Diomed." Gretorix moved around his master's room, clearing away the books and scrolls left by his readers. "It reminds me of the day that I sailed away from Britain with my lord Justus. There were cliffs there, where we at last left the shore, and as we stood out to sea, the sun caught them and they glittered so that I was almost dazzled. And there was a green rim of grass along the top. It was the last I saw of Britain." He paused a moment. "Those gleaming cliffs sinking into the sea. This new palace of the Emperor's, my young lord, is just the same. Like gleaming cliffs rising from the Palatine. But the people are very angry."

Diomed smiled a little.

"Gretorix, since you have been my slave, I swear I know more of Rome than when I had my legs. Why are the people so angry?"

"Well, when the Emperor began to rebuild their houses so quickly and well, and showed them his plans for all the fine new streets and parks and squares, they were willing to forgive and even forget that they thought it was he who burned their city. Now they growl and murmur again that they were right in the first place, and he burned it only that he might take half of it for his new palace. The parks and gardens for it cover half the middle of the city."

Diomed's eyes grew dark as they always did when there was any mention of the fire. It had taken him long, weary months to get better from his fever, and ever since he had been silent and withdrawn. Only Gretorix could bring a little life into his face or kindle in him the faintest interest in the world outside. Nor did he ever speak now of Peter.

"Don't press him," Justus had said when Gretorix told him of this. "Don't press him. He will come back to it himself."

But Diomed did not come back, although he did nothing to hinder the Christianity of his slave. He knew well where Gretorix was going when he allowed him to slip off secretly when the lamps were lit, and Mancus safe past on his nightly round. In his mind he followed him on all he could remember of the journey down through the dark city and along the Via Ostia, packed now with the wagons of builders rumbling into Rome, and into some crowded chamber there in the dark streets of the tombs, where the sign of the fish would have been painted on the door.

But when he tried to picture the face that Gretorix would see there, he could remember nothing. He could only close his eyes on this unutterable sense of loss which never left him, and hide from Pallius and Melas his weak tears of longing for something he still did not understand.

He knew where Gretorix went also when the lady Pomponia swept in in the mornings with all her ladies, swirling her black draperies and telling Diomed cheerfully that she had permission from his mother to borrow his young slave. She would smile at Gretorix, for deep affection had grown between these two. They were both British and both Christian. They would go out, Diomed knew, and outside Pomponia would dismiss all her ladies except her beloved Mary, and on to Gretorix's willing arms they would load big baskets of food and comforts and medicines. By the small back ways they would go down into the parks and gardens and open spaces of the city, among the shacks and tents that sheltered the homeless people. And the lady Lucina, the Light of Christians, would go among them about her work. And he knew who else would be there also, giving his strength and faith for the comfort of all who needed it.

But he could no longer ask Gretorix about Peter. He remembered clearly the dark, terrifying cellar of Simon Magus, and the fear and weakness that had torn his faith to shreds. Now he could not even speak of it, for to speak of it would be to face the fact he could not bring himself to look on. He might never get another chance.

Through the long months of his recovery and the building of the Golden House above the heads of the fretting people, his friends came and went, and sat below his couch. The Praetor Justus Gallius, when he could spare time from his splendid duties; the lady Pomponia; Demetrius the sculptor, though he had no work to do now, and his long, fine hands lay idle in his lap. No one had left Rome this summer, for the Emperor was too busy with the furnishing of his new palace. So through the long, hot days when Pallius and Melas stirred the air above his head with the soft tremble of feathers, they talked to Diomed of this and that, idle chatter to cheer a sick boy, and, with all of them, his heart ached to hear the one name he would not ask for.

In the Villa Verius these months passed in uneventful peace, and even the anxious face of Justus began to smooth itself out as time went by. But among the homeless and workless who wandered hungry about the city, standing for hours in silent groups to watch the rising walls of the Golden House, anger was spreading, like a great festering sore, against Nero Caesar, who would take so much and let his homeless people starve.

Frantically he cast about for ways to please them and win back their favor. Time was running out, and he was ever conscious of the watching face of Tigellenus at his shoulder —like a cat who has trapped a mouse within a hole and waits with endless patience for its victim to come out. He dropped all his work on the finishing of his palace, and at immense expense he rushed men and materials from all the other sites to put into some order the charred and blackened shell of the Circus Maximus. Feverishly he urged them on, and when it was at last completed, he staged a Circus for his people, the greatest Circus that even he, their generous and extravagant Emperor had ever given them. How could this fail to still their muttering and growling—these citizens of Rome, who loved the Circus as they loved life itself?

Day after day it went on. First, the thundering day of chariot racing, with dust rising like smoke above the blackened arches of the Circus, and the crowd standing screaming in their seats in a frenzy of excitement. Athletic contests followed, and the skills of wild, dark Thracian horsemen, dodging the thunder of demented bulls until the moment came to kill. There were gladiators in hundreds, fighting real battles, leaving the yellow sand bestrewed with dead, or in single, desperate combat for death or glory. African elephants charged each other and locked their gigantic tusks, goaded on to fury by the thrusts of spears, and savage beasts from the jungles of the hot south were turned loose on the gladiators marked for death. In the soft air, scarlet ribbons fluttered and lifted in the curls of the white-clad slaves who moved among the crowds with sherbet, iced fruits, and long, cooling drinks. When the days grew hot, a thousand hidden pipes sprayed the air with a mist of icy perfume, and past the yelling crowd raced the leader of the Games in his golden chariot, crowned with laurels, tossing numbered balls into their frantic hands. To those who caught one, the Palace Steward would give a prize next day—a piece of fine furniture, a slave, silver, or even a small house in the hills. Gifts from the generosity of their Emperor.

"Hail Caesar!" they cried in the long, wild excitement of the Games. "Mighty Caesar! Divine Emperor!" Clutching their lucky balls they waved and shouted to their benevolent Nero, and from his draped and flower-decked box he smiled and nodded his pleasure in their happiness.

But when the Games at last were over, and they turned for home, there was no home. Only a fast-decaying hovel in some public park, and a packet of sherbet or a sugar cake that died quickly in the stomach of a hungry man.

In the end there was no more money for Circuses, and the grumbling in the hungry city was rising to a snarl. Always in Nero's anxious mind was the knowledge that no one had yet been found guilty of the fire of Rome. If he could not keep his people happy, then their thoughts would turn inevitably back to him. Up in his Golden House, gleaming in the sunshine on the crest of the Palatine, he sat among the gorgeous riches of his treasures and gnawed his nails until they were eaten to the quick, and his pale, protuberant eyes were full of loneliness and fear.

Tigellenus looked at him and gave no help.

"They desire, Divine Caesar, that someone be held to blame for the burning of their city."

"Well, who?" Nero's voice was querulous. "Who? Who am I to blame? The police are no help."

He looked into the cold eyes opposite his own, and saw in them the same accusation that lay in the eyes of his people. Indeed, he suspected deeply that this "friend" of his had helped to put it there. Tigellenus did not answer him, and Nero looked at him for one long, appraising moment, then flung out of the room, clacking through the ornate corridors in his high-soled sandals, between the grounding spears of his guards, to the apartments of his wife Poppaea.

Later that evening, he called a meeting of his Council. The shadows were creeping between the dark green marble pillars of his Council Chamber when a strangely bland, elated Nero took his place at the head of the long table where the members were already gathered. As he sat down, he did not look at Tigellenus on his left, and at the bottom of the table was a new figure to the Council; the leather armor and the dark heavy face of the Chief of Police.

He did not waste any time. As soon as they were all seated again, he burst out with what he had to say to them, and he could not now restrain a bright, triumphant glance at Tigellenus. He had discovered, he said—and his words fell over themselves in his hurry to place another neck in the noose that had so nearly caught his own—he had discovered who had caused the fire of Rome. Through all these long, anxious months he had never ceased to make inquiries on behalf of his outraged people, and now he was certain where to lay the blame. He looked along the expectant faces and the rising murmur of interest around the long table. He gave a little giggle of uncontrollable excitement.

"The Christians!"

What he had not expected was the torrent of agreement that fell on him at once, which amazed and silenced him. From all sides of the table they agreed with him, and rose in their seats to join in his accusation. The only one who did not speak passed unnoticed in the noise.

"They are slaves and low-class foreigners who teach equality. They will destroy the social system!"

"They teach of a Kingdom greater than the Kingdom of Rome!"

"They sang hymns of joy in the streets as Rome burned!"

The Chief of Police struggled to be heard. The Emperor would be amazed, he said, if he knew how many converts had been made in the Palace itself by this man Peter, and his friend Paul.

Nero looked from face to accusing face, almost light-headed in his relief that he had laid the blame so easily.

"In my Palace! They will be the first to go! Arrest them both!"

"Certainly we will take the man Peter at once. But Paul of Tarsus is not in Rome. He has been long expelled from the city for sedition, and his life is forfeit if he returns."

The yellowish face of Tigellenus was like a mask of wax. Around him, in the voices of the assenting counselors, his bright hopes for the throne of Caesar crumbled into nothing. After all his careful plans and the long months of waiting, the Emperor had found himself a scapegoat, and one that seemed to please everyone. Disappointment was sour in his throat, and thwarted hope sharpened the bitterness of his malice against the man who had refused to help him in the beginning.

"Divine Caesar," he said. His cold voice cut across the hubbub. "Most of these Christians are, as you say, foreigners and slaves. But some are not. Some are Romans in high places. These, I think, should be made a special example to our people."

"Yes! Yes!" Nero was beside himself at the success of his idea. Clever, clever Poppaea. She had said all this to him before, but he had not listened. "Yes, indeed. If there are Romans of rank found guilty at this trial, then they will be used as an example to the people of Rome, to teach them not to meddle with false gods! We shall offer their punishment as a sacrifice to Jupiter in atonement for the tragedy of Rome!"

"Trial?" Tigellenus picked out the word carefully. "We cannot try them all. There are thousands. Let us only try some of the leaders, and then we can round up the rest for general sentence. We will call upon the citizens of Rome to tell us everything they know."

Long after they had left, Nero still walked restlessly about the lofty room in the deepening shadows. His fingers were twitching, and his pale eyes were alight, his artistic mind busy on all the glorious details with which he would embellish the punishment of the Christians.

The quietest of all the men around the table had been the first to leave, slipping unnoticed out a side door of the Golden House, and sending his body slave urgently for his horse. Where he might be seen around the Palace, and in the center of the city, he kept to a sedate pace, answering the respectful salutations of the citizens. But when he reached the quiet streets of the lower slopes of the Viminal, he spurred his horse to a gallop, his purple cloak flying in the wind, and his panting slaves left far behind him. As he passed through the great outer gates of his house, he shook his head a moment at the golden fish that marked the pillar, and then flung himself from the horse and threw the reins to the bowing Steward. In the quiet, flower-filled atrium he shouted at the first passing slave.

"My wife!" he cried urgently. "The lady Petronilla. Bid her come to me at once. Quickly, boy, quickly!"

When she came, smiling her welcome, trailing her bright skirts across the colored floor, he took her by the shoulders and looked a long moment into her lovely, tranquil face before he could bring himself to speak.

Thus it was that when the shadows were deep in the valleys of Rome, and only the last light lingered among the first stars above the hills, two men stepped out into the darkness from the side gate of the House of Pudens on the Viminal. They turned at once into the small dark lanes that led downhill between the great houses. Neither of them was young; one was tall and heavy-shouldered, leaning on his staff, his gray hair blown like a cloud in the soft wind. The other was shorter, slighter, with a bundle of scrolls held awkwardly in his hands as though they had been gathered up in haste, and a case of tablets underneath his arm.

In the city, the police were moving through the streets in squads, nailing up notices on the doors and walls. The Christians, they read, were to be arraigned for trial for the fire of Rome. They asked all citizens to come forward with what evidence they could provide.

Chapter 11

The next afternoon, the lady Pomponia came to call upon the lady Gallia, her fair face carefully calm among all the excited chatter of the ladies of the House of Verius and their friends, who were hot with the latest news from the city. The Christians, it seemed, had burned Rome to make way for their own kingdom. There was no longer any doubt of it. The city was in an uproar, and people flocked to every police station through all the fourteen districts, falling over one another to pour out their tales of the night the flames took hold of Rome.

Pomponia clasped her hands in the folds of her soft black

robes and listened as tranquilly as she could. This was the reason why she had come to the Villa Verius. Here she could hear all the gossip of the enemies of Christianity, and learn more than even her husband and Petronilla's could whisper to her at the end of their long official days. Through the laughter and chatter and the tinkle of the wine cups, she listened carefully for anything that might help her friends. Peter and Mark were safe. Word had come during the morning that they had reached their long-planned hiding place, safe only because the Prefect of Rome himself had rushed hotfoot from Nero's Council to warn Petronilla of their danger, and bid her get them into hiding. Pomponia pressed her hand a moment to her fore-head, and felt the flower-filled room grow dim with the tension of the path they all must walk.

"My dear Gallia." She laid her crystal wine cup, un-tasted, back on the table and stood up. "My dear Gallia, you will forgive me leaving you so soon. But we have guests this evening and I must be ready for them. And I would like to visit a little with the boy before I go."

The younger woman looked peevish and pettish, broken in the middle of the most exciting gossip since the fire, but Pomponia's smile was firm and tranquil.

"He is poor company, I tell you," the boy's mother said irritably. "I don't know what has come to him of late. He can barely bring himself to speak to anyone except that British slave of his."

"All the more reason to cheer him with a visit."

Firmly Pomponia moved toward the door, and reluctantly the lady Gallia rose in courtesy to go with her to Diomed's room. In the peristyle and along the columned colonnades, the warm, golden sun of the late summer lay like a bene-diction, and the gardens were warm and heavy with the peace of the season.

Down in the city the police were overwhelmed. From

all corners of Rome the population rushed to inform against the Christians, and in the hovels in the parks, in the poor quarters that still stood unharmed across the Tiber, families clung close together in the dark and dingy shadows of the houses; and wide eyes looked at each other in terror and waited for the banging on the door. But the police were not concerned with them yet. They would start with a handful, whose guilt they could prove, and then they could arrest the masses who would need no trial.

In all the police stations they set up trestle tables and gathered all the men they could spare, a scribe with tablets at the side of each. Outside they held back the struggling, shouting crowd that filled the narrow streets—the same crowd who, a few days before, had shouted at their Emperor for the selfsame crime of which they now accused the Christians. One by one they let them in, each pouring out his story for his own reasons of hatred and jealousy and fear and superstition, and the terror of something larger than himself. Death to the Christians! Wide-eyed and excited and gabbling, they told their tales of what they had seen or what they thought they had seen on the night the fire began. In the packed streets, while they waited to get in, their stories grew in the talk and the excitement and the heat of the September sun. Here and there a cold-eyed, quiet one would stand and wait among the crowds, walking quickly in to the waiting police to tell his tale of sober facts, conscious only of his virtue, his faith in his own true gods, and his sense of public duty.

Despite the floods of talk, by afternoon the list of those they really wanted, and could accuse with reasonable evidence, was still a short one. One name stood high on it, and when he looked at it, the Chief of Police shook his head. He rubbed the dark stubble on his fleshy cheeks thoughtfully and shouted for his horse.

"I'll not take this one on my own authority," he said.

He found Tigellenus in his new office in the Golden House, where all the maps and charts had been replaced with one vast plan of Nero's grand new Rome; it covered a whole wall in colored marble, threaded with all the beautiful streets that were yet to come.

"Ah," said Tigellenus when he saw his caller. He sat himself behind his long mosaic table. "You have had a successful day?"

"Well—yes, my lord. I know, my lord, that Nero Caesar said that the example must come from his own palace. But, sir—" His heavy face was uneasy. "There is one name here on which I'm reluctant to take action. This man is loved in every corner of the Empire. My lord, I don't think Rome will stand for it."

He put his parchment down before Tigellenus, and his stubby forefinger laid itself against a name.

"He is too much loved, my lord," he said again, unhappily, and from his troubled face it seemed he was not only thinking of the feelings of the people of Rome.

"You have evidence against him?"

"Oh, yes, sir. First-class evidence. Conclusive that there was something odd in what he did that night. But to set fire to Rome? Sir, I tell you frankly I am not sure of it."

In his eyes lay the puzzlement of long experience that told him that despite the evidence, there was something wrong in this. Something too glib and perfect in the tale that had been laid before him. But the hard-eyed fellow who had told it had laid his oath. He shrugged helplessly, and Tigellenus raised his eyebrows.

"I see no problem, my friend," he said. He tapped the parchment in front of him. "There is the name. You have your evidence, and what is more, I am willing to confirm it personally. Make your arrest. It is people of this rank who must set an example to the citizens of Rome. If they fail, then they must pay for it."

The Chief of Police sighed so long and deeply that all the leather of his armor creaked and strained like a frigate taken by a squall.

"My lord," he said resignedly, then saluted and was gone.

Pomponia still sat below the gold and purple flowers of Diomed's couch, struggling to kindle a spark of life in the pale and indifferent young face. Gretorix was not attending him, and while the bored and restless Gallia drifted about the room, bidding the boy sharply to show his visitor more interest, Pomponia did not dare to ask his master where he was.

Diomed knew nothing of the attack upon the Christians, and his mother did not care. So it seemed to Pomponia that the fear that hung in the warm, golden light of the September room was all her own, rising to desperation for the friends of whom all her light talking could get no news. In despair she folded her headscarf closer over her graying hair and prepared to take her leave.

"Diomed," she began. The bronze doors flew open with a crash, and Gretorix was within the room, sweat standing clear on his forehead and in the damp curls of his hair, his breath whistling through his throat. His blue eyes were wild and wide and full of horror. Before he could even speak, he collected himself under the scolding of the lady Gallia, bowing over his clasped hands and closing the door behind him. He managed then to gasp his apologies, and took his place at the head of Diomed's couch, sending Pallius and Melas from the room with a flicker of his eyes, which came back then to rest dark and appalled on the lady Pomponia, beseeching her for some help, and looking out of a face as white as the walls of Nero's Golden House.

Pomponia knew the sick certainty of the catastrophe she had feared. Who was it? Her husband and Petronilla's should be safe; they were not themselves Christians. Could Peter and Mark have been found? Whom had they taken?

With dry lips she answered as best she might the fretful talk of Diomed's mother, complaining of his poor looks and lack of spirit, while tension rose to fill the painted room until even Diomed grew aware of it and his dark eyes flashed from the face of Gretorix above him to that of Pomponia, now as pale as the slave's.

Gallia halted by the door in her restless drifting.

"Pomponia, forgive me. I have to dine tonight at the Golden House, and I need time to dress. Will you forgive me if I leave you? Diomed, care for your guest and see that savage of yours cares for her also." She looked at Gretorix in distaste. "And see he cleans himself up, or I will have Mancus do it for him. Forgive me, Pomponia."

Pomponia stood up and took her farewell as calmly as she could, hoping the other woman would not feel the trembling of her body as she kissed her. Gretorix sprang to open the bronze door into the sun-drenched colonnade, and Gallia called for her servants. The door was closed again, and Gretorix whipped round, his back against it.

"My lord Justus," he cried, and his voice was hoarse with anguish. "My lord Justus! They have taken him! Like a felon to a common prison!"

"Tigellenus," Pomponia said, and said no more.

"Who? Why? Who has taken Justus Gallius?" There was life now in Diomed's voice, and fear. "Who has taken him, and why?"

Pomponia moved to him quickly, her hand at her throat.

"You should not know of these things, Diomed, my son."

"Yes he should!" cried Gretorix. "Yes he should! He knows where my lord Justus was on the first night of the fire. So do I, but I am a slave and my word is nothing. My lord Diomed, you will tell!"

Pomponia looked in mounting confusion from one boy to the other.

"How? What can he know, tied to this couch?"

"My lord Diomed, you will tell! I will take what comes to me for my part of it!"

Diomed was almost as confused as Pomponia.

"I will tell anything that need be." The late, soft sun was bright beyond the windows, and the appalled and frightened face of Gretorix was ashen in the shadows. Diomed looked at him beseechingly. "First, I beg you tell me who has taken my lord Justus, and why!"

Pomponia strove to calm the two of them, speaking as quietly and steadily as she could against the sick fear that rose in her for her old friend and the many more who must follow the same road. Gently she told Diomed of the Emperor's order that the Christians be found guilty of the fire.

"Though why they take Justus Gallius I cannot think. He was at Anzio on that night. This the Emperor knows."

"My lady Lucina," Gretorix said, using her name among the Christians. He moved slowly from his place against the door, as if he were suddenly weary. His eyes were fixed on Diomed, even though he spoke to Pomponia. "My lady. On the first night of the fire, my lord Justus was not in Anzio."

It was Diomed who told the story of that terrible night, but even he still did not speak of the fear and horror of the cellar of Simon Magus. Before the firm and gentle eyes of Pomponia, who had for half her lifetime walked in fear and danger for her faith, he could not bring himself to say that one short hour of fear had cost him his. It was enough to tell, with the fierce, anxious face of Gretorix urging him on, that Justus Gallius had been at the gathering on the Via Ostia, and had brought them back into the already blazing city.

"There were many, many people there, my lady. Many must have seen him there all evening."

Pomponia drew her veil close about her head in tension and anxiety.

"But Diomed, my son. They were all Christians. Who now will listen to a Christian?"

There was tense and anxious silence in the room, and the bright birds glowed sharp behind the still, dark figure of Pomponia. Her loved face had grown pale and old.

"You alone can save him, Diomed," she said. "He is in danger, great danger, no matter what we do, but at least we may prove that he did not hold the torch that kindled Rome."

"What of Gretorix, my lady? I cannot pretend that I went out alone. What of Gretorix?"

It was Gretorix himself who opened his mouth to answer, but before he could speak, the bronze doors crashed back once again, and their startled eyes turned on Mancus the Steward in his brown tunic; bright, malicious pleasure glittered in his eyes, and behind him in the golden sun the round, unfeathered helmets and the leather breastplates of police.

"There!" He stood aside to let them in. "The slave! Couldn't hide what he had been about that night. His hair charred to a cinder and his clothes all burned. Christians! What is wrong with the God of Israel?"

His thin, dark face was working with hatred and satisfaction, and small specks of spittle collected at the corners of his mouth.

"Take him!" he snarled.

Two of the police leaped forward and seized Gretorix, and began to drag him from the room before the lady Pomponia found her voice.

"Stop!" she cried then, and all the authority of the lady of Pomponius Aulus Plautius was in her voice.

The two police stopped and looked from her to their officer, Gretorix dumb with surprise between them.

"Officer, explain this. This slave is mine. I have only lent him to this household. I demand to know what you are doing!"

The officer was unimpressed. Lady of a Consul she may be, but he knew she was just another of these Christians, and it was only a matter of time before they got them all. He ground his spear on the colored floor and looked at her easily.

"Charge of incendiarism, like all the others."

"On what evidence?"

Almost idly he consulted a paper tucked into his belt.

"Deliberately started a fire in a cellar down an alley near the Circus Maximus. First-class, direct evidence."

Pomponia glanced despairingly at the two boys. This was not in the story she had heard. She looked helpless and distraught, and across the room Diomed looked at Gretorix, suddenly small and young between the two men. Simon Magus! Here was the ending to that moment of lost faith and fear and despair and foolishness. Oh, God of Simon Peter and Justus and Gretorix, what had he done?

"It is not possible," he said suddenly, loudly and firmly. "It is not possible. This is my body slave, and on the night of the fire he never left my side. And all Rome knows I cannot leave my bed. It is not possible, and through my father, I will swear this in all the courts in Rome."

The police looked at him in a moment of doubt and disbelief, then looked at their officer. Mancus lost his look of pleasure and his face grew ugly with malice and frustration. Pomponia and Gretorix looked at Diomed in astonishment and affection, thinking what this might mean. Mancus recovered first.

"We will see about that, my young lord. You may take him away."

Gretorix was hustled through the door into the middle of the squad that stood outside. The sun had moved from the back courts now, and he was pushed out into the shadows. The corridors were loud with the tramp of nailed boots and the clang of spears.

It was some moments before Pomponia could speak.

"My son," she said then, gently, "this is a lie that will take strength and courage to endure. Have you enough?"

"I have enough." Diomed's face was the color of the pillars of his room, and his eyes were black with pain. "I have enough for Gretorix. Did I not fail him on that night? Like Peter, who denied his Master," he added softly. "But, my lady." His voice was thick with misery. "Do you not see?"

He told her briefly of the encounter down in the dark alley near the Circus, and the moment of weakness and faithlessness that had made him turn to Simon Magus.

"Do you not see how I have to pay now for that moment? My lady, I will swear my life away for Gretorix, just as he would have given his that night for me. It will mean nothing, for I know now that the gods I will swear by are no longer mine. But, oh, my lady, if I am to swear that Gretorix was not out that night, I can do nothing for Justus Gallius! My lady, you see? I cannot help them both."

In the long minute of grief and silence in which they looked at each other, the firm scuff of sandals was heard again along the colonnade, and once more Mancus stood in the open door. His dark face was evil in his satisfaction and his certainty of success.

"I will arrange for Pallius and Melas to have care of you," he said coldly to Diomed, "and inform your lady mother on her return from the Golden House." He turned to Pomponia, and his voice was savage. "There is another," he said, "who has your patronage. The great sculptor, Demetrius." He shot a vicious glance at the boy. "No one will be able to swear away his guilt. I saw him myself, creeping along the walls of the house on the night of the fire. Sneaking away from the flames he had kindled in the stables. The police are looking for him now, and it will not be long. Rome looks for the death of these fiends. It will not be long."

Diomed closed his eyes on the clang of the door. Demetrius too? How much he bore the guilt for. How different it might all have been if his faith had only been strong enough to bid Gretorix run when they met Simon Magus. To have come to Peter, believing, and so have walked home. Justus Gallius could have ridden straight back to Anzio and been undiscovered. Demetrius would have raised no fire. And any part that Gretorix played would have been a thousand times forgiven. He moved his weary head and opened his eyes to Pomponia, who bent above him.

"My poor son. I must go. I must leave you. We are all in terrible danger, and I must do what I can to help. God be with you, and I will come again soon."

Pallius and Melas stood back to let her through the open door, bowing their heads above the bright, embroidered badge of the House of Verius that blazed across the breast of their tunics. When they came in, Diomed looked at them, but did not dare to speak and ask them what they knew. But they drew close and stood one at each side of the head of his couch, then turned together to look at the bronze door. Melas spoke.

"My lord Diomed," he said. "You are not alone."

"We have kept our secret," added his twin, "but now it is your need to know."

He put his hand down the front of his tunic under the brilliant badge of Verius Bautus, and pulled up a piece of cord. On the end of it hung a small silver fish. He looked down at it, and the face of his brother opposite him echoed the same peace and pleasure that filled his own.

"Peter gave it to us himself," he said, and his voice was soft with reverence and awe.

Chapter 12

They threw them all into the prison on the Capitoline; scores of them were huddled together in sweating, dank stone cells that were built for half a dozen. All day long the passages echoed with the tramp of boots and the clang of doors, as fresh victims were thrust in among the rest. In the overcrowded cells there was a strange exalted happiness. The Christians were to be tried for their faith even as their Lord had been before them, and they turned to Him gladly to accept it. The long, dark, vaulted corridors were filled with echoes, and the hollow murmur of prayers beat back a hundredfold, washing like an unheeding tide over the marching and shouting of the guards. Now and again some prisoners would begin to sing, women's voices rising like bells up into the gloom of the sweating vaults, and one by one they would all take it up, a wave of faith and exaltation surging through the crowded prison until even the guards fell silent and looked at each other uneasily in the shadows.

Here Gretorix was brought, fearful and yet elated. He had known, as they all had known in Rome, that his life might in the end be the price of his faith. He was not afraid. He knew nothing for himself of the sick fear and horror that he had known when he heard they had taken Justus Gallius. As he was hustled through the jeering, crowded streets in a roped line of prisoners, he tried to think of what Diomed had said before they dragged him out. Would he have the strength to endure the lie? And if he did, what of his lord Justus? Gretorix groaned aloud, and beside him a policeman turned and laughed, mistaking his anguish.

"That's right! Better groan now, boy, while you have breath! By the time Nero Caesar is done with you, you will not have much to groan with! Christians!" His face changed, and he leaned over and spat at the boy.

He did not want his life at the cost of his lord's. But he was helpless. Helpless. Everything now was in the hands of the frail boy in the painted room which already seemed like another, half-remembered world.

In the airless, crowded cell, he could at first neither see nor breathe, crushed between the icy stone of the walls and the press of hot, weary prisoners still lifting their eyes and voices to the one small grating above their heads, looking at the light of day and pouring the testimony of their faith out into the astonished streets of Rome. Gretorix leaned against the wall and choked back the sickness in his throat, fighting the panic that rose to a shuddering tide, washing over him in an ice-cold trembling as the great bolts shot across the door outside. Desperately he looked up at the blue September sky which glowed through the grating, hidden every so often by a curious face that bent to peer at the captive Christians—to jeer or spit, or merely turn and walk away. He was not afraid to die. He had thought of that too often. And to die was merely to enter into that Kingdom of God which Peter taught them they must keep always in their souls here on earth. He had thought often of death. But he had not thought of such things as this monstrous, crowded, evil-smelling darkness, with no air to breathe and the whole, bright world reduced to a square of blue far up above his head, a great studded door bolted between him and the rest of it. He closed his eyes and felt the sweat all over his body, no colder than the icy wall behind him.

A firm hand closed on his arm.

"Steady, my son, steady. You will get used to it."

The voice was calm and quiet above the singing.

He did not need to open his eyes to know who it was. He kept them closed until he had mastered his thickened throat and the hot tears risen in his eyes.

"My lord Justus," he said then. "I disgrace you."

"No, Gretorix, no." The older man was easy, calming. "You are young and alone. The first clang of the door is always the moment of terror. Even for me. Yes, I assure you," he said to the boy's movement of doubt. "Even for me. But we are both past it now. Come, tell me all you left behind you at the Villa Verius. And who betrayed you?"

Gretorix grew calm and forgot his terror, telling the dim face beside him in the gloom of all he knew. The lady Pomponia had been there when he was taken. No, he did not think that she was threatened. But they were looking for Demetrius. He had heard no word of Peter and Mark, but, surely, if they were taken, it would be all over the city.

"As it is with your arrest, my lord. Someone has seen to it that you are condemned before your trial, and the people are shocked that one they so respected could be so base. My lord, you must have enemies."

He could just see the tranquil nod of the gray head.

"Yes, I have enemies."

"But you have friends too, my lord. My lord Diomed would have told everything to save you. He would have sworn to where he was on the first night of the fire, and that you were there also. But now, now, my lord—"

He turned and laid his head on the cold wall behind him, and Justus waited patiently.

"Now?"

"Do you not see, my lord. He cannot save us both. It is you or me. He must either say that you were in his company on the Via Ostia, and let me go, or he must swear that Simon Magus lies, and I never left his room. He cannot save us both." The eyes he turned back on Justus Gallius were wide and stricken in the gloom.

Justus was unperturbed and his voice was gentle.

"When you get out, I charge you to tell your young lord that even in the world I go to, I will not forget he would have done this for me."

"But, my lord, he may still do it. How can we know? He may save you and let me go. You are Romans both."

The boy caught the momentary flash of the man's teeth.

"No, my son. Diomed will save you, if he can save anyone. And I am quite sure—" His voice changed. "I am quite sure that if he finds the strength to save you, he will in time find the strength to save himself." He paused a moment. "And it will not all have been in vain."

Up in the Villa Verius, Diomed had made his choice, gathering together all his frail strength for the fight to save his slave. He began with his mother, who would not listen to him, laughing away the idea that any efforts should be made to bring back the barbarian she had always detested.

"Nonsense," she said. "Xania can supervise Pallius and Melas. They grow quite sensible. You have no need of that savage. And a Christian as well!" She picked disgustedly at the gold paint that chipped from the ends of her long nails. "A Christian, and a criminal! We are all fortunate not to have been burned in our beds! No, my son, you are well rid of him. And when I think of that man Justus Gallius, so close to Nero Caesar, and plotting all the time—! I have spoken sharply to Pomponia because she brought such creatures to our house. Now I must go. The Emperor wants our advice in planning some particularly splendid gala. Forget this boy, I bid you."

Diomed refused to eat. He turned his head resolutely away from the twins when they brought his meals, and they did not press him, their eyes meeting his in quiet complicity in what he did. With empty faces they reported the untouched food to the lady Gallia.

"What do you *want?*"

She was shrill with irritation. Nothing so annoyed her as to have the smooth, luxurious routine of her days disrupted by the unreasonable nonsense of her son. "What do you *want?*"

"I want my father," he said, "who is a Magistrate. And I will swear by any gods he chooses that Gretorix never left my bedside in this room that night."

His mother fluttered and twittered and twitched at the colors of her flowing robe.

"It is nonsense. Rubbish. Mancus saw him covered with burns. And the great Simon Magus himself took the trouble to swear that he followed him down into his cellar and attacked him there. He left him unconscious in the middle of a mass of burning coals. When he came round, the cel-

lar was alight. And this was right beside the Circus. The
boy was obviously one of the incendiaries. A Christian—
there is no doubt of his guilt. Really, Diomed, I have no
patience with this nonsense. You must leave these things
to us. You do not understand."

The boy's face was white and tense and very firm. I do
understand, he thought to himself with relief, that the
pride of Simon Magus has been too great for him to admit
that I was there, and that he failed to heal me. That is
something. It is a little easier.

"You will not bring my father?"

"No, of course not. He would be very angry."

"Well, then, I will die." His voice was calm and even.

"What!"

"I will die. It would be very easy, my lady mother." Suddenly he sounded unutterably weary. "Do you understand
how little there is for me to live for? I could so easily die.
Just loose my hold. That's all I have to do. Just loose my
hold."

His mother looked at his pale, transparent face on the
color of his pillows, and in a moment of sudden anguish
she saw that this was true. Life in Diomed was low. He
had never really recovered since his fever at the time of
the fire. He could easily let go. Whatever her faults and
her foolishness, she loved him, her only child. After one
long look she put her frantic fingers to her mouth and ran,
calling for the slaves to find his father.

His father was annoyed. He rarely came to his son's
room, and saw no reason to be troubled now. And Mancus
the Steward stood inside the door, sullen and amazed to
find so helpless a hand raised to fight him. They stormed
about below him where he lay on his high couch, silent
and white-faced and obstinate.

"I say that Simon Magus lied," was all he would say.
"And I say that Mancus was mistaken. He was overexcited

on the night of the fire, and thought everyone to have been there. Gretorix was not burned. He was not out. Choose your gods and I will swear by them."

Mancus' dark face was risen with a sullen flush, and his thumbs twitched about his belt as he stared at the boy, but in the presence of his parents he could not even speak. Diomed stared steadily back.

"Mancus, poor man, was overexcited, and imagined this."

"This man Simon Magus is important. He amuses the Emperor. How am I to brand him a liar?" His black-haired father paced the colored floor, angry and baffled as a baited bull.

"I will swear it. No need to say he lies. It was some other boy."

"No! No, no—you are mad, my son. Your illness heats your brain. I will not do it."

"Very well. I will die."

The cool voice halted his father halfway to the door, and, turning just as his mother had done, he too saw how easy it would be for the boy to fulfill his threat. The lady Gallia burst suddenly into tears, and Verius Bautus threw up hopeless hands.

"Very well! Very well! I will see to it. Beg the Emperor's indulgence."

"And, my father—"

"What now?" The black curls were shaken low upon his father's forehead, his small eyes bewildered. The bull was cornered.

"I want your promise that when Gretorix returns, he will suffer at the hands of no one." He looked straight at Mancus. "No one in this house. Your promise, my father. You will protect him."

"I will do anything for peace." Verius Bautus looked in exasperation from his pale, threatening son to his sobbing mother. "Anything! Now, is this nonsense done? Never have I known such uproar for one slave. I would buy you twenty more instead, and better."

"I want Gretorix."

"So I see." His father snorted and was gone.

Mancus bowed the lady Gallia out the door behind him, and as he stood straight again, Diomed looked at him innocently.

"Mancus," he asked, "have they found Demetrius yet?"

The bronze doors closed with a crash that shook the swooping birds, and Melas and Pallius drew close with grins of triumph on their dark faces. But Diomed had closed his eyes, and his lower lip was tight between his teeth.

"My lord, what is the matter? You have won. You will get him back."

The boy opened his eyes.

"Yes, but, Melas." He turned his head aside. "To get him back, I had to let another go. There is nothing now to save my lord Justus Gallius."

A few days later, Gretorix came back to his young lord. But there was no cheerful greeting between them. Both of them were too aware of the price that had been paid that he might walk again in freedom through the streets of Rome.

"And you will be safe, Gretorix, no matter what they do to the Christians." Diomed's mouth was twisted with distaste. "Nero Caesar was amused at the devotion shown to his slave by a poor cripple. He did not know my father had a crippled son. He found it funny." He sighed, and his young face looked old and bitter. "It may be if he laughs at such as me, he finds more hope for himself."

They were both silent. The shadows of the autumn day hung around the pale walls and dimmed the colors of the flying birds, and the first cool air touched their quiet faces.

"The nights grow chill, my young lord," said Gretorix

absently. "Soon we must shutter your windows." But the minds of both of them, no matter what they said, were on the gray-haired man whom Gretorix had left behind him in the crowded, stinking prison underneath the city streets.

He was tried a few weeks later with all the others against whom they had found evidence. Most of the accused were slaves or low-class Romans, but here and there among them were the white robes of the wealthy and the purple stripes of rank. Among the women was Mary, beloved handmaid of Pomponia. In the face of Aulus Plautius, they had not dared to take the mistress, so they had taken the maid instead.

For hours before the opening of the trial, the people flocked in hundreds up the beautiful broad white marble steps of the Basilica Julia. The court was packed with eager citizens, crowding the benches, standing on each other's shoulders, and clinging halfway up the pillars, by the time the Prefect of Rome, Titus Flavius Sabinus, took his place behind the high seat of judgment. He stood awhile and looked down with eyes of confusion and pain on the crowd of helpless people whom he must try for nothing more than that they held the same faith as his beloved young wife and her gentle, black-robed mother. He sighed, and those close round him saw him shiver. He passed a hand across his face and took his seat.

"Let the trial begin."

His eyes had cleared. His face was calm and impassive, his fine, intelligent glance roaming dispassionately over the scene below him. He was the Emperor's servant.

It did not take long. One after another, the witnesses poured out their stories. They had seen this and this and this. Christians with burning brands before the fire began. Christians who danced and sang through the flaming streets. Christians who refused help to the trapped and the dying. All the things that Justus had seen, and feared as he had seen them, through those dreadful flame-filled days and nights. And all witnesses were willing to testify that the Christians preached a Kingdom that was greater than the Kingdom of Rome.

Against the Praetor Justus Gallius, the Commander of the Praetorian Guard himself gave evidence, moving from the high seats beside the Prefect in all the gold and silver splendor of his uniform, and telling of how, in the hour of Nero's need, the prisoner had been found missing from his post, and had been seen beside the Circus Maximus in the first hour of the fire. He was a known Christian, a follower of Peter, and could have had no purpose in leaving Anzio that night other than to assist in the firing of the city. So said Tigellenus in his cold, satisfied voice, and he did not look at Justus Gallius; no one dared to contradict him.

Under his hard, expectant eyes, and the expectant eyes of the people of Rome that packed his court, the Prefect brought himself to his judgment. He turned his mind from Petronilla and Pomponia and the possible consequences of what he must say. He was the Emperor's servant.

It was plain from all the evidence, he said heavily, and kept his eyes on his parchments, that to be a Christian meant to be a revolutionary. Their aim was the destruction of the Roman kingdom and the establishment of a new Kingdom of their own. The punishment for treason was death. So must the punishment of Christianity be death.

Judgment was given, and the police began their task of rounding up the known Christians. In the next anguished days, thousands and thousands of poor helpless creatures were driven from their homes, guilty of no crime except that they believed in God. Through the city streets they were herded in their masses, until every prison in the city was crammed to its reeking walls, and the dungeons under the two Circuses could hold no more.

On a still, soft night a few weeks later, the autumn moon hung enormous over Rome, and the clouds were mild and white above the pale splendor of the hills. Diomed could not see them. For some reason, although the night was warm, Gretorix had insisted on fastening the shutters across the windows before he went out somewhere. He grew fierce and wild when Diomed objected, and wearily his master let him have his way. Now in the close-shuttered room there was silence. Diomed was tired, and had sent everyone away save Pallius, who stood against the wall behind him, for he must never be alone.

If he gave idle thought to Pallius at all, it was to assume that he stood behind him in the manner of a waiting slave —against the wall, his arms folded on his breast, and silent until his master spoke. Pallius stood indeed against the wall, but his rigid hands were clasped one upon the other round his secret silver fish, and his eyes were closed in a young face taut with suffering. His lips moved without pause in silent, anguished prayers.

For hours there was no sound. Diomed dozed against his bright pillows, and wondered idly where Gretorix had gone. Behind him, Pallius prayed in urgent silence. The birds swooped forever on the painted walls, and no breath stirred the quiet lamps. In the warm silence, petals dropped one by one from a bowl of scarlet flowers and lay like blood upon the colored floor.

Gretorix opened the door quite quietly, but with a fixed, stunned look, as if he had small idea what he did. In the same numb, quiet way he reached up and shot the heavy bolts. Diomed opened his eyes and Pallius took one step toward him from the wall. Slowly the boy came across the floor and paused at the steps below the couch, and his strange still face began to crumple.

153

"Diomed," he said hoarsely, and his master's eyes flew wide. "Diomed." His voice cracked on the second word, and he flung his arms out wide, facing his young lord with a look of such naked agony that Diomed cried aloud. Then Gretorix collapsed, flinging himself up the shallow steps to bury his head among the golden flowers and fringes of the counterpane, clinging to Diomed's unfeeling hands and torn with sobs that shook him as if to wrench his bones apart.

"Pallius! Pallius, what is wrong with him?"

Pallius knelt down beside him, and his arm was firm around his shoulders, but he did not try to speak to him. For a moment he laid his own head down in a gesture of hopeless grief on Gretorix's shoulder, then he lifted it and spoke to their master.

"My young lord," he said. "Bear with him. He did not want you to know. He has been down tonight to the Vatican Circus, where they are executing all the Christians. He hoped to see his lord. Perhaps at the end to speak with him."

Gretorix flung away his protecting arm.

"I saw him," he gasped, and the tears flowed so fast he swallowed them as he spoke. "I saw him. My lord Diomed, I must tell you. I cannot, but I must. I must tell someone. Oh, my lord Diomed!" He covered his face with his hands as though to shut out the sight, yet he must speak of it or lose his mind.

"They took them, thousands of them, and soaked their clothes in pitch. Then they tied them up on poles and planted them along the avenues of the Vatican Gardens. Thousands of them! Along the paths and in the groves and round the Circus." His voice rose. "And when it came to dusk, they lit them! Torchlight for great Caesar's gala! But of this—oh, my young lord, I cannot tell you!" He dragged

154

his fingers down his face, shapeless with grief and horror. "They screamed," he said, almost quietly.

"My lord Justus?" asked Diomed through dry lips.

"My lord Justus." The agonized voice fell to a whisper. "I found him. I spoke to him a moment while there was still time. He was at peace, and thought the price of the Kingdom of God still not too high." He flung down his head again on the golden flowers, and his voice came muffled. "Then they lit him. I ran away. I could not look. I ran away. Thousands of them. They were all the same." After a while he grew calmer and lifted his head again. "They sewed others into skins of animals and herded them along the avenues, then they turned the dogs on them. And through the roads of flaming torches, Nero Caesar drove laughing in his chariot, dressed as Apollo, with maidens driving before him to strew his path with flowers. He is mad, my lord Diomed, mad." Now he could hardly speak, lying against the side of the couch, worn with grief and shock. And it was Diomed the helpless who took charge firmly, bidding Pallius to send Melas into him, and himself take Gretorix to his quarters and give him hot, spiced wine and stay with him until he slept.

"Gretorix," he said softly as the boys went out. "You have no news of Demetrius? You did not see him?"

"No, my lord Diomed. No news."

"Or of Peter and Mark?"

"No, my young lord." The hoarse voice spoke with an effort. "I have not spoken with the lady Pomponia. It is safer if we Christians keep apart. But I would have heard in the city, I am sure, if they were taken. They are safe."

Diomed let him go. He felt himself ashamed. Tonight had seen a dreadful, vicious death for Justus Gallius and thousands more who had done no more than follow the God of their belief. Yet, secretly, deep down, his horror was laid over by a sweet, urgent relief that in the killing of the Christians, Peter had escaped.

All these had died for their faith. Surely he could have the strength to live for it. And while Simon Peter was still alive, there was still hope for him.

Chapter 13

Now there was uneasy peace in Rome. For long after the massacre of the Christians, it was as though the city lay in stunned silence, save for the fanatics who had laughed and danced along the lanes of human torches, and who now slapped their thighs as they sat around their wine cups, rejoicing in every dreadful detail they could remember of Nero's grisly gala.

But gradually the common people came to life again and remembered the things that had been done. They had risen in fear and superstition against the Christians themselves, but now in the booths and taverns they whispered more than ever against their Emperor, saying that the dreadful killing of the Christians had been no just punishment, no matter what their crime, but only the crazy satisfaction of the bloodlust of a mad ruler. The grand new avenues were spreading daily farther through the ruins of Rome, filled with the clamor of building, so that the rows of new houses sprang up almost overnight, and tall apartment blocks rose to hide the dark groves of the hills. Yet, the people were not content, and the tide of their murmuring rose up to the Golden House, and in his vast rooms of unimaginable splendor Nero stalked between his treasures with empty eyes and gnawed his stumps of nails and wondered where he had gone wrong.

The religion of the Christians was now forbidden. They met together under pain of death and were not allowed to practice or speak of the things of their belief. The big killings were over, but every little while, to enliven some entertainment for their harrassed ruler, the police would swoop on some small band; and their agonizing deaths would bring light and interest for a little while to Nero's brooding eyes.

These were lonely and quiet days for Gretorix and his young lord, and Diomed often looked back and thought to himself that his life was now exactly as it had been before that hot spring day when Demetrius had first spoken of Galilee. He was kept occupied by his readers and tutors, and his visitors and the tedious, patient labors of his dumb Fuscus. He had not known then that his world was empty. Now he looked forward almost in desperation to the snatched moments when he could talk to Gretorix and to Melas and Pallius of the things that had grown to be everything to them all. His days of silence and withdrawal were over, and he grudged that the moments of talk were few and hedged with fear. Mancus was hostile and suspicious, watching all who came and went into the painted room. If he could find three proven Christians there talking of their God, then not even Diomed could save them from a gaudy death to cheer the empty lives of Nero and his friends.

Pomponia came rarely now, and for this Gretorix was almost grateful. In her aged face and the snow-white hair that had so recently been only touched with gray, he saw the echoes of his own grief, and the horrors of the dreadful night that would not leave his mind. She was very careful. If she called on Diomed at all, she came only with his mother, and took care that they were never left alone.

Months had passed, and they had not exchanged a word alone, and Gretorix was desperate to speak with her, to ask the question he dared ask of no one else. She saw it in his eyes and avoided them, talking quietly to Diomed and the lady Gallia of the small things of their daily life, the teaching of his tutors, and the building of the new Rome. And when she left, Gretorix would look at his young lord and lift his shoulders helplessly, and Diomed's face was resigned and disappointed. He was even more desperate than Gretorix to ask the question.

It was high summer again, and the bronze doors open to the shadowed colonnade, before they got their chance. Mancus the Steward bowed in the curtained doorway, his bright, dark eyes flickering over the group inside the room —the two ladies sitting below the steps, the soft folds of their robes flowing into the sunlight on the colored floor, and the lady Gallia's gold-tipped fingers raised to hide a yawn. Gretorix stood against the wall behind the couch, his arms folded and his eyes watchful on Pomponia. Above Diomed, Pallius moved the scarlet fan against the heat.

Mancus wanted the lady Gallia. If her ladyship would be pleased, her silk merchant waited in the atrium with the silks she had commanded. They were newly come in a caravan from Persia. There was some query, if her ladyship would—"

"Oh, my Persian silks!" The lady Gallia was on her feet at once, her pretty painted face alive, all boredom fled. "Forgive me, my sweet Pomponia. A moment and I will be back. No, no, don't come." She held out her hand as Pomponia moved to rise, and threw a glance she could not hide at the plain black robe. "It would not interest you. Come Mancus, you will need to pay him. Diomed, care for your guest till I return." In a whirl of excited draperies she was gone, and after one sharp glance around, Mancus followed her.

Defeated, the lady Pomponia sank again into her chair, and for a moment, no one spoke. Gretorix moved swiftly over to the door, and looked up and down the colonnade. Then he turned back to tell Pallius to be gone.

"No, my sons," Pomponia said before he could speak, and she looked round at all three boys. "No. You must not ask me the question I see in your eyes. You must not ask me."

Gretorix was sidetracked.

"You know about the twins?" he asked, surprised.

She smiled at Pallius, bringing back a trace of her old beauty, and Gretorix was struck afresh that old age had so taken her in a few short months.

"I know."

He returned to his question.

"Why may we not ask? We are Christians. His secret is safe with us."

"I know that, Gretorix. I know that. But you are in a dangerous house. Mancus is forever on the watch, and what you do not know, you cannot tell. I would not burden you with this secret."

She looked at the boy's dismayed and mutinous face and went on gently.

"It is hard for all Christians now, Gretorix. And danger-ous. For the moment we must endure and keep our faith living solitary within ourselves. This I will tell you. Simon Peter is safe and well hidden, and he is no longer alone. His dear companion, Paul of Tarsus, whose life is forfeit if he should set foot in Rome, has braved this decree to join him here in his time of danger. We have a secret place where Christians not so dangerously placed as you may still gather and hear them preach. But you I dare not tell, you are too well watched."

"Paul of Tarsus?" Diomed spoke from the couch. "No one has told me of him. Is he another of the Twelve?"

"No, my son. Watch the door, Gretorix. He is a Roman citizen. He was an unbeliever who preached most bitterly against God, until God himself struck light into his eyes. Now, like Peter, he has preached and taught in every known corner of the Eastern world. In some happier days, I will tell you more of him. He is the friend of Simon Peter. Now do not ask more, my sons, because it is not safe for any of us."

Gretorix moved from the door on slow, reluctant feet.

"He must be well hidden," he said grudgingly. "The po-lice are combing the city for him this year gone."

Pomponia smiled suddenly, a smile almost of real mis-chief that lit her face and killed the lines of grief.

"Yes," she said. "The police have been very busy. He is well hidden."

When Mancus came back, escorting his lady, he could not see that they had moved since he had gone. Gretorix stared impassively from the wall, and the brown face of Pallius was idle and empty below the feather fan. From her chair on the floor, the quiet voice of Pomponia told them of the beauties of a new fountain, set playing yester-day by Nero himself, in one of the fine, beautiful squares of the new Rome.

Under his calm face, Gretorix seethed with frustration and disappointment. He was only half a Christian who was not allowed to set eyes on Peter and sit below his chair to listen to his teachings of his Master. And deep in his secret heart, he still hoped to do something to help his young lord. But Diomed was calm. To him of late had come a strange, uncomprehended patience. He was waiting quietly for something. He did not know what.

Up at the Golden House, as the summer drew to its dry, exhausting end, a limping figure in a blue robe sought audience with Nero Caesar. He did not get beyond Tigellenus, who eyed him cautiously across his table. Tigellenus did not trust this man, yet, like all pagan Romans, he was afraid of him.

"Yes?" he said, in answer to the deep and over-respectful bow. "What can I do for you?"

"My lord Commander." Simon Magus leaned eagerly on the cold edges of the marble table, and his dark eyes were a little wild. "My lord Commander, I bring you a plan to smoke out this traitor Simon Peter, and the other, Paul, whom I hear keeps him company. All this time, the police have searched and searched and cannot find them. Yet I, the Magus, will bring them out, my lord Tigellenus. They will come to my call."

Proudly he reared up and stuck his thumbs into the girdle of his robe, and the light glittered in the grease on his black hair.

Tigellenus was noncommittal.

"How?"

Simon Magus bent again, close and confidential.

"I will issue them a challenge, my lord. I will perform the greatest feat of magic that the world has seen, and I will challenge them that their God can not prevent me. They will come. They are afraid of me, and they will have to come out of hiding to stop me proving to the citizens of

Rome that my magic is indeed stronger and greater than their God. They will have to come. Then you can take them."

Now Tigellenus was more alert. Nero Caesar was bored, his new palace almost complete, and he was restive and discontent under the cold eyes of his people. Suspicion had come close to Tigellenus over the fire, and he did not feel too sure of his own safety. Often now he felt the eyes of his Imperial master fixed on him in cold distaste, and when the Emperor was bored, heads were apt to fall. He seized on the chance of some fresh entertainment, even if it did not succeed in flushing the Christian leaders from their hiding place.

"What is this magic feat?"

"I would fly."

The face of Simon Magus was bland and yellow and self-satisfied, looking calmly down on the astonishment of Tigellenus.

"I would fly. And before the citizens of Rome, I challenge the God of these Christians to stop me."

The Commander stood up and paced the floor below the vast mosaic map, and now his eyes were bright as the magician's own. Here might be many fish in one net. A new amusement for his bored, capricious master; and if the Magus should succeed, and the Gentile God be held to ridicule, then Rome was done with Christianity. A certain alarming sympathy for Christians was running through the city, and it would be quenched forever. Then there could be added the public execution of the leaders, who, as the Magus said, would have to leave their bolt-holes if they were to be able to defeat his magic. Excellent. Excellent. Excellent. He clapped his hands together in satisfaction. This had everything to recommend it. He could not wait to tell the Emperor.

Nero was delighted. He would attend the contest personally, and it would be held in the Circus Maximus, where all Rome might have space to witness the final defeat of these presumptuous Christians. Then! The pale eyes shone with anticipation. Then there could be another gala for the execution of their leaders. Eagerly he called in his Treasurer, and laid vast wagers on the success of Simon Magus.

"I am afraid, my young lord." Gretorix paced backward and forward like a caged animal below Diomed's couch. "I am afraid for Peter and his friend. What can they do? If they do not come, then Christianity in Rome is dragged at the heels of Simon Magus for the world to laugh at. And if they do come, and Peter uses his power to stop this monstrous magic, then they are both dead. My lord Diomed, it can't fail, either way. And there is nothing anyone can do."

"This is exactly what the Magus planned, Gretorix." Diomed spoke slowly and thoughtfully. "That, for him, it cannot fail either way. He is as clever as he is evil. No wonder Nero Caesar laughs and claps his hands for he must feel that this delivers him all Christians in Rome, and their leaders with them."

For a moment there was no sound but the lisp of the boy's sandals up and down the floor, and then Diomed smiled.

"Gretorix," he said, "it comes odd from me to teach you faith, but can we not just wait and leave it in the hands of Simon Peter?"

Gretorix looked doubtful and unconvinced.

"I agree, my young lord, because I see nothing else to do."

"Tell me of it."

"Oh, the proclamations are up all over Rome, for a contest between Simon the Magician and Simon of God. All Rome is invited, and the great tower from which the Magus will fly rears itself into the sky above the Circus walls. He preens himself around the streets among his followers as though the contest is already won."

"There is only one more day to go? And no word to anyone from Peter as to what he means to do?"

"No word. I have had no chance to speak to the lady Lucina, but I have asked secretly among the Christians in the city, and no one knows anything."

"You must be early tomorrow, Gretorix, to see it all and tell me everything. I will arrange it."

Gretorix was early, elbowing his way through the dark, sandstone passages into the glare of sun inside the huge bowl of the Circus itself. In the curious, talking, jostling crowd, he was edged up the steep, worn steps to the seats at the very top, where slaves might sit. Even here, the tower of Simon Magus reared above him, high into the pale, tranquil blue of the autumn sky, dwarfing the distant hills and making nothing of the tall, golden stylus that marked the center of the arena. Around and below Gretorix the benches filled up steadily with the chattering, speculating people, and through the waiting hours he stared until his eyes were sore, trying to see the gray, balding head that must tower above any other there. But he could see no sign of Simon Peter.

At long last, when every seat was full, and the people packed standing in the sand itself, the silver trumpets blared in the sunshine, and the crowd rose to its feet as Nero Caesar strutted to his golden chair.

The trumpets blared again, and beside the Imperial Box, the challenge was read out. By the strength and virtue of his magic, Simon Magus would fly from the top of this tower down into the arena, and he challenged Simon Peter, the leader of the Christians, to come forth and, by the power of his God, prevent him from so doing. Tier upon tier of whispering faces craned and stared down into the empty half of the arena. But the soft sunshine beat down on the yellow sand, and no sandal stirred it. Gretorix was torn first with relief and then anxiety, and he remembered the words of his young master. "Let us leave it all in the hands of Simon Peter." He calmed himself, and then smiled to think that his lord Diomed should be advising him to faith.

A rustling gasp stirred the huge crowd, and Gretorix looked up to the top of the tower, shielding his eyes against the sun. The man must have been there all the time. He had seen no one go up. Now he stood poised at the edge of the platform, great clumsy wings fastened between his body and his arms.

"Come forth!" he screeched. "Come forth!" In the silence his voice was as thin as a bird's, and even at the distance Gretorix could see the wild glitter of his dark eyes. "Come forth and show the powers of your God! Stop me, Simon Magus, who shall fly, if you are able! Come forth and stop me!"

Gretorix glanced down into the arena below. No one came.

"Then I fly," screamed Simon Magus. "I fly and no God can stop me!"

The crowd shrieked as he leaped, and scrambled to its feet, watching the few desperate seconds of hopeless flapping and then the long, agonizing fall of the screaming puppet until it crashed into shapeless death on the sand below the tower.

A terrible silence took the people. They stared across the arena at their Emperor, who stood as they for one wild, silent moment, staring back, before he turned and flung himself away through the door at the back of the Imperial Box, followed by his Court, who turned only to throw their last bewildered glances at the broken body that no one would run to help.

Gretorix pushed his way downward among the hissing, whispering, wondering crowd, staring desperately all around him, struggling to get down into the open corridors where he might run more freely among the people to find the one he sought, if only to look at him. It could betray them both to speak to him. His eyes were not on the steps, and he would have stumbled and fallen were it not for a firm hand that gripped him by the back of his tunic and hauled him up.

"Go gently, young friend," said a familiar voice softly. "He is not here."

Gretorix struggled round and looked into the eyes of Demetrius, his wild hair close-cropped and a bushy beard hiding half his face. Before the boy could speak he laid a finger on his lips.

"No better hiding place than a vast crowd," he said again softly. "But not if we shout each other's names."

The boy's eyes were filled with pleasure at finding him safe, but his mind was on Peter.

"How do you say he is not here?" he whispered. "He has defeated the Magus. He must be here!"

Demetrius smiled through the soft beard.

"Where is your faith, my son?" he said, and echoed Diomed. "There was no need for him to come. They prayed, he and Paul, where they are. Prayer was quite enough, and faith. They did not need to come."

Gretorix knew a moment of shame and confusion that his still-pagan lord had somehow understood this, and he had not. Then he turned back to Demetrius.

"Where are you? Where do you hide?"

Demetrius spoke close beside his ear.

"In a secret chamber among the tombs along the Via Ostia. We are several there, and safe."

"Peter?"

They struggled to hold together as the crowd pushed down from the last few steps into the dark, vaulted corridors. Demetrius smiled and laid a hand on his arm.

"No, Peter is not there. Nor can I tell you where he is. But I see him, and he is well and works still for all Christians as best he can."

The crowd was thinning as they came toward the great archway that led into the sunlit street. Without another word, Demetrius slipped away from him and vanished among the frightened and marveling people.

Chapter 14

It was two years since the windy night when Rome had blazed into the racing sky, and still Simon Peter was not found. To the charges of treachery and incendiarism that lay against him, they had added that of causing death by sorcery, the death of Simon Magus. The authorities of Rome dare not admit the power of God—only that Simon Peter may have had greater power in the Black Arts that Simon Magus practiced. Thus were the frightened people calmed and reassured, and the Christians branded as sorcerers as well as criminals.

In the great house on the Esquiline, life was tedious and dull. Gretorix grew to despair that he would ever see the face of Simon Peter again, and struggled to keep alive a faith he could not practice, and which he could only speak of in the utmost secrecy. He had not seen Demetrius again, even though he had gone wandering recklessly at night through the cities of the dead, creeping with silent feet along the soft grass of the avenues of tombs, searching in vain for light or life. He had seen nothing and learned nothing, and when at last he came away, he cursed himself for a fool. Knowing the habitations of the dead to be the meeting place for Christians, the police had combed them from end to end, looking for Peter. They had not found him, or Demetrius, or anybody else. Why should he hope to succeed where they had failed?

Wearily he turned home and trudged up the dark hillside, reproaching himself for a faith so weak that it perished in loneliness, and thinking about the strange new tranquillity and contentment of his young lord. He seemed to have a faith these days stronger than his own, and to be forever looking forward to something, whereas Gretorix could only look back and long for what he had lost.

On a high morning of brilliant summer, when the very air seemed to tremble in the heat above the tree-crowned hills of Rome, he walked idly along the small road below the back walls of the Villa Verius, coming back to the slaves' entrance from an errand for his master. The dust of summer was hot and dry upon the roads, and he scuffed up idle clouds of it with his sandals, watching them rise about his feet with eyes as empty as his mind. His name was spoken twice before he heard it, and he turned in surprise to the man who called him from the same small grove of olives where he had stood on that long-distant night with Demetrius, after he had brought Diomed up from the flaming terror of the city. A pang of misery struck him for

Justus as he thought of it, that he could not have died there that night, unknowing, in peace.

"You called me?"

The man's face was familiar, and Gretorix frowned in an effort to remember him. An upper servant, not a young man, with a shoulder knot on his tunic in the colors of some great house.

"Quickly, boy. We have no time to waste. It is luck I caught you so soon. Do you not remember me? I am the Steward of the House of Pudens."

"Ah." Gretorix looked again, and interest kindled in his eyes, remembering the night he had been caught peering in at the love feast. Now he well recalled the round, brown, quiet face. The man drew away from him a little, moving deeper into the sun-flecked shadows of the trees.

"You know me now? Good, then you will trust me. I have a message for you from the lady Lucina, and to prove I tell you truth, she sent you this." He put something into the boy's hand, cold and smooth as silk, and Gretorix looked down at the small carved fish of palest jade which Pomponia had always worn around her neck.

"She is well?" he asked, suddenly anxious.

"She is well herself, boy. But she needs you to go on an errand for her. There are few we can trust within the city. The young lady Petronilla is sick to death, and my lady Lucina wishes you to go to Simon Peter, to beg him that he will come to heal her."

"She sends *me?*" The boy's eyes were amazed and startled on the man's face.

"Yes, quickly. Yes. The lady dies, and there is little time."

"But why me?" Gretorix could not accept that after two long years of hopeless questioning, they would send him now and tell him where to go. The Steward grew impatient, tapping irritably on the rough bark of the tree beside him.

"The lady Lucina trusts you. There are many reasons why she thinks you best, but no time to tell them. Is that not enough?"

The boy looked down at the smooth, small fish, warming in his palm, and when he looked up his eyes were bright.

"It is enough. Tell me."

The man peered round him in the shadowed grove before he spoke.

"Go out the Via Appia, about a mile and a half. You will come to a place where the hills draw close above the road, and a small spring pours from the rock. There is a bench there where travelers may rest and take a drink; you cannot miss it. Behind the spring, a mulberry tree grows close into the rock. Watch carefully, and when you are sure you are alone, lift the branches. You will find an opening beneath them. Go in there, and you should find Peter. Give no messages. Tell him yourself who needs him—it is safer."

Gretorix would have turned and run at once, his breath already short with excitement and a little fear. After two empty years, he was to go, not to stand on the edges of the crowds, but to look into the face of Peter and speak with him, alone. The man seized him by the wrist.

"Calm, boy, calm. Or you will run yourself and others into danger. I had not finished. If Simon Peter is not in the hill, then go on a little way and you will find a house. Ad Catacumbas, it is called. The Steward of the lady Lucina will be there, and if you show him the fish, he will let you in. There you will certainly find Peter. But be watchful. Just beyond the house there is a large police station."

Obediently the boy steadied himself, and for a fleeting moment recalled the small smile on the face of the lady Lucina when she had said the police were very busy looking for Simon Peter, but he was well hidden—beside them.

"Go now, son, and God be with you."

The Steward moved off across the hill, and Gretorix paused a moment in the gray shadows of the olives, wondering if he should tell his master where he had to go. Then he also turned away down the hill. Better be beaten when he came back if Mancus had missed him, than burden Diomed through the long day with his secret.

The sun was high, and the shadows of the tamarisks were small and black along the sides of the hot paving stones of the Via Appia. By the time the hills were folding close, he was warm and thirsty. He looked with pleasure at the small, clear spring of water that tumbled down the rock face beside the road, tinkling into a pool where tall ferns clustered at the water and the small flowers in their shadow were blue as the hot sky. The stone bench along the curve of the hill beside the spring was empty, and Gretorix reached for a cup and held it in the icy trickle. The water was cold like pain inside his throat, and from the short, thyme-scented turf on the hill above his head, the larks hurled themselves up singing into the summer heat.

He drank and looked across at the mulberry tree that sprawled on the other side of the spring. Suddenly his hands were icy as the cup he held, and the stricken trembling of his knees had nothing to do with his long walk. He put down the cup and clasped his hands together to still their shaking, and then took them apart and looked at them in fear. All the times he had been close to Simon Peter in the crowds were nothing. The man I will speak to now, he thought, will have touched the hands of the Son of God. In the silence and the sunbaked shelter of the hill, with the light brilliant on his face and the larks shrilling in the idle sky, he knew suddenly the awesome truth of all he thought he had believed before, the reality of Jesus of Nazareth, the Son of God, who had walked the earth so recently in Galilee, and of Simon Peter, whom He had named the Rock—the Rock upon which God would build his Church. Fear and awe and knowledge too great for understanding beat about his head, and he leaned his forehead against the wall of rock and shook as though he had been taken with a fever, staring dumbly at the water running through his fingers, and hearing from another world the clear singing of the larks and the hum of bees in the crimson flowers beside the road. He clasped his cold, wet hands across his face and turned to fly.

Then he remembered who had need of Peter. His errand was not his own. And how could he forsake Lucina, the Light of Christians, who had never herself forsaken the poorest Christian in Rome who needed her. Slowly he steadied himself and calmed from his sudden panic.

Yet, as he looked carefully up and down the road before he lifted aside the branches of the mulberry tree, he was still trembling, and it took all his courage to step into the cool dimness of the cave behind the sheltering leaves. It was not quite dark; the sunlight filtered through the leaves behind him, and there seemed also to be light ahead. He felt his way carefully along the walls, cold and rough beneath his doubtful hands. His heart thudded with the burden of his secret. All Rome searched for the hiding place of Simon Peter. Instinctively he looked back, but there was nothing there except the dark masses of the mulberry tree and the sunshine, golden and unreal behind its leaves.

The first chamber he came to was empty. And the second. But in the walls of this second one there were new-made graves, rough platforms scooped out of the rock face of the chamber. Here the Christians had laid their dead in nameless graves, in secrecy and safety, marked only with their emblem of the fish. The chambers, like the passage, were not quite dark. Light seemed to come from above, and Gretorix guessed that narrow openings in the roof must lead right up to the top of the hill; they were screened perhaps with trees. The air was cool and still. He turned from the graves and went on into another passage that led from the second chamber.

This one was longer and quite dark, but he could feel cool air moving against his face and he went steadily on, stumbling on the occasional loose stone and trying to hold his balance where he could see nothing, leading himself with his hands along the walls. His eyes had grown used to the dark and he was moving more surely when, quite suddenly, the passage turned. There was a pale, growing glow of light, and in a few paces he was out into the third chamber. His hands still outstretched on the walls beside him, he stood and gasped.

The green, solid-looking hill must be as hollow as a bubble of blown glass! This was why they called the Villa Ad Catacumbas, The Hollows. This great cave was big enough to hold a thousand people, and it must be here the lady Pomponia meant when she said there was still place where Peter could preach and teach in safety. But the vast cave was empty now. Through it all glimmered the same unearthly green-gold light that had filtered through the leaves of the mulberry tree, but here and there the sun fell through in beams as sharp and clear as spears, picking color from the bare, pale rock, and falling like a white light around the one solitary empty chair.

It stood alone on a little rise at the far end of the huge cavern, plain and simple and too large for the ordinary man. It seemed to the nervous boy to symbolize all that Simon Peter was—too great for any ordinary man. He felt again the surge of awe and panic he had felt beside the spring outside, and turned quickly before it took a grip on him, feeling for the jade fish beneath his tunic. He must go to the house. Behind the tree, he was compelled to wait in fretting impatience while two travelers rested themselves against the wall on the stone bench, swallowing cup after cup of the cold, welcome water and complaining to each other of their taxes.

When at long last they were gone, and he was free to go on down the road, the first brilliance of the day was over. The shadows lengthened and grew soft, and the colors of the flowers were muted, and on the hill above, the slopes of grass were golden in the passing light. The boy began to run. It was all taking too long, and he would never forgive himself if he were too late.

At the gates of the Villa he had difficulty in getting even as far as the Steward. The porter told him to be gone and quick about it before he set the dogs on him, and the massive wooden door was closing in his face. Just in time he noticed that the porter's eyes were on his tunic and the house badge of Verius Bautus on his breast. Fool that he was! What better way to get thrown out of the house that sheltered Peter? Quickly he tore the cord from round his neck, and thrust a hand through the closing gate, the jade fish lying in his open palm. The wood crushed hard against his wrist, but the door stopped and then opened just a little, and the porter peered out.

"Why did you not say?" he said. "Come quickly."

He stepped aside, and Gretorix slipped through the narrow gap. He looked carefully up and down the road before he closed the door again.

"Now. Your business."

"With the Steward. From the lady Lucina. I can see no one else."

"H'm. All right. Wait there and I'll get him."

The white-haired Steward listened carefully to Gretorix and weighed the jade fish in his thin, old hands.

"Can I not give the message?" he asked.

"I was told to give it myself. If Peter consents to what it asks, then you will know."

"Very well." He looked down at the fish again. Gretorix

felt it bore a stronger message to him than any words of his. "I will take you to him. He is in the garden—there is a secret entry there to the caverns in the hill. But, my boy, if you have bad news for him, be gentle." The thin, old face was tender, as if he spoke of a child. "He is old and he is ill. Do not blunder in with the rough words of your youth."

Gretorix had no thought of blundering. His mouth was dry and his knees trembled again uncontrollably as he followed the old Steward across a circular, pillared drawing room with a wide, tessellated floor of tender green. He stood back then and let him walk alone down three curved marble steps into a sheltered garden, taken like a bite out of the smooth green hill that rose behind it.

It was another of the hollows, making of the garden a deep, secret cup, guarded by the house. The bare rock of its sides were soft with trellises and arbors where the roses poured in fragrant showers, filling the sheltered air with perfume; the soft rushing of the fountain barely drowned the humming of the bees. The sun was held as a crystal cup would hold the pale light of Falernum, and in its golden glow, an old man rested on a marble bench. His gray head leaned back among the roses, and his big, clumsy hands were folded in his lap.

Gretorix walked across the marble paving of the garden with leaden legs. Then he fell upon his knees, and his eyes were hot with some half-understood dismay; he was torn with confusion that the Rock of God could also be an old man resting in a garden, weariness in every line of his massive body, and sickness in the deathly pallor of his face. Awe was gone now, and fear. Only a desperate love held him, for all that Simon Peter stood for, and an agony that it must be he who would speak the words to drive him from his gentle shelter and out into the hostile streets of Rome.

He did not remember much about it afterward. A hazy memory of the scent of roses and the sun warm upon his back, and the unutterable sadness of the mild, dark eyes that opened on his own. Then the tired old body he had come upon, gathering quietness and strength as Peter heard where he was needed—the deep, quiet voice thanking him for coming in such danger with the message, and the hand of Simon Peter on his head and the blessing of God.

Somehow he got himself out of the garden.

They gave him wine then and something to eat, and told him to get back into the city with all possible speed and tell the lady Lucina that Simon Peter would follow and be in her house at sundown.

It was late into the night when he at last came back to the Villa Verius, walking like a boy asleep, his head bent from the lambent sky and the stars that blazed above the sleeping city. It had been long arranged that if any one of the Christian boys be missing, then the others would unbolt the small back door. He went in this way now, walking like a shadow through the colonnades and turning the handle softly on the bronze door.

Diomed was awake, waiting for him, Pallius standing by the wall, but after one look at the white, quiet face he spoke gently, wondering if the boy would even understand him.

"What, Gretorix? What is it?"

"They have taken Simon Peter."

His young face was old with the fears and strains of his long day, and his voice flat with pain. Diomed's eyes grew dark and sharp, and Pallius moved unbidden from the wall. Once again, Diomed the helpless took control, hiding the sick and final dismay with which the slave's words had struck him like a sword.

"Bolt the door, Pallius, and then pour him some wine. Now, Gretorix, slave or no slave, I bid you sit. It is a long day since you took a book to be mended for me in the fourth hour. Sit there and tell us all that has happened."

In one of the ivory chairs below the steps, Gretorix sipped unseeing at the cup of wine, and told them of the message to Peter.

"Ah, ah," said Diomed. "And they took him on his way to Petronilla."

"No, no. It was not like that." Gretorix shifted in his chair and thought of the crowded atrium of the lady Pomponia's house, hushed with anxiety and grief, where he had hung about unnoticed all the evening, listening for news. "He came to the Villa Pomponius quite safely. He came alone. He wanted no one, he said, to suffer the danger of his company. But he would not heal my lady Petronilla."

He looked up at the gasp from the other two boys.

"I know. His little Petronilla. His daughter in God. He bade her mother heal her grief and let her go. It was her time, he said, to go to the Father, and he must not interfere. The lady Petronilla is dead."

He paused a moment, remembering the amazement and shattered grief that had run through the packed atrium, bowing their heads like a wind through barley on a hill.

"Then, it seems, they all spoke to Peter—all those who loved him. They told him he was not safe enough where he was, and that for the sake of all Christians, he must preserve his life and go to some distant place of safety. I think that were he not so tired and sick, he would never have listened." He closed his eyes a moment against the weary old face among the roses. "But they persuaded him. They sent a horseman to Ad Catacumbas, and arranged for a carriage to come from there along the Via Appia to pick him up. He left the Villa Pomponius, again alone, and walked out to meet it. He was leaving Rome."

He got up and roamed restlessly around the room, looking at nothing, as if he could not find words to continue.

"You know why," he said at last, and kept on walking. "You know why they say Peter always looks so deathly sad. Because he denied his Master thrice, and no matter what has happened since, even though his Master has forgiven him, he can not forgive himself."

"Yes."

"Well." He drew a sharp breath and shook his head. "This is what I have heard, and it is all over Rome." He spoke slowly and carefully, as if he must do so if he were to speak at all. "Tonight, they say, Simon Peter left Rome along the Via Appia, to meet the carriage that was to take him safely away from fear of death. There is a place on the Via Appia where the road rises a little and the shadows of the tamarisks are close beside it. I passed it today. They say—they say that as Simon Peter reached that point, he saw the night grow strangely brighter. In this unearthly light, his Master, Jesus of Nazareth, came toward him on the road. And Peter, amazed, leaned upon his staff, and said to Him, 'Where goest Thou, Lord?' And his Master gave him answer that He was going into Rome to be crucified again."

There was a pause as he walked the bright floor, and then he turned again to the wide, waiting eyes of the other two.

"Peter understood that this time the cross was meant for him. Nor did he now deny his Master. He turned and the vision faded away into the night. Simon Peter came back along the Via Appia, and into the center of the city. Within an hour he was arrested. All this I have heard among the slaves in the house of Pomponia, but tonight Rome does not sleep, and in the streets they talk of nothing else. Simon Peter will be crucified."

He fell silent, nor had the others anything they could say. The wide windows were unshuttered against the hot night and beyond them the stars paled against the lightening sky. From some small farm beyond the city, in the middle of their stricken silence, a cock crowed into the coming dawn.

Chapter 15

The next day, Paul of Tarsus followed his friend in along
the Via Appia and gave himself to the police. They lodged
him in prison as became a Roman citizen, but for two long
months Peter lay alone in a stinking dungeon in the Tullianum, lowered through a hole in the floor like an animal,
into a den below the level of the city sewers. For their
trial, the sad, harassed face of Titus Flavius Sabinus pre-
sided once again over the packed, excited benches of the

Basilica Julia, and up in the Golden House, Nero's eyes were bright with anticipation.

The trial was short. Sedition, incendiarism, and causing death by sorcery. Each charge alone claimed Simon Peter of Galilee for the degradation of a felon's death. Paul's life was forfeit when he walked into the city. Within the hour they were condemned to death.

Gretorix tried to keep the news from Diomed, but he saw it in his pale and tragic face, and wrenched it from him; his own dark eyes were sick with sadness and final disappointment.

"And when?" he asked. "And when?"

"Tomorrow. At dawn. In the Vatican Circus." Gretorix could barely speak of it.

For Diomed, this was the end. He had lived through these last months in some strange patience, waiting for he knew not what, calm and certain that this time when the moment came, his faith would not fail him. Now there would be no moment. He had grown to blind faith that Simon Peter could reach to anywhere and somehow beat down the pagan walls of the Villa Verius with Christianity and healing, so that he might walk again, and walk in the name of the God he now believed in. Now, tomorrow, Simon Peter was to die. The walls of his father's house and the helplessness of his own body closed round him afresh like a prison as dark and dreadful as the crawling dungeon underneath the Tullianum.

It was a long, silent day. There was nothing they could find to talk of except the one thing of which they would not speak. With the coming of dusk and the lighting of the lamps along the painted walls, a silent Gretorix helped Diomed with his evening meal, lifting his eyes to meet those of Melas behind the couch as the boy drank down his cup of wine. Soon they stood together, watching him as he drifted into sleep.

"I gave him twice as much of the potion as Xania bade me give him for a restless night," said Gretorix. "He should sleep now until morning—when we are back."

"He will be all right?" Melas was a little doubtful.

"He will be all right. What can happen to him, poor boy. Every Christian in Rome will be on vigil tonight, and it is kinder that he can sleep it through. Come. Is Pallius ready to go?"

It was dark when Diomed struggled from a thick and stupid sleep. Two of the lamps had failed along the wall, and the room was faint and shadowy in the pale light of the third. Beyond the windows was black night with neither moon nor star. Layer upon layer of sleep rolled back, and Diomed came to recognize his room.

"Gretorix," he said, and his voice was hoarse and stupid.

"Gretorix," he said again into the silence, and then "Pallius! Melas!"

The one dying lamp flickered in the air from the windows, and the painted bird on the wall above it moved and trembled, watching him with its bright eye.

Panic struck with ice-cold sweat across his head. The terror that had haunted him all the long years he could not walk was with him now, in the familiar room that changed with the flickering shadows and the silence into a place of crowding horror from which he could not move because he was alone. He was alone and he could not move. He should never be alone. They had been told that under pain of death. He should never be alone! He closed his eyes against the shifting shadows, and his mouth opened in a scream for help. Then he remembered. This was the night that Simon Peter was to die. If the boys were gone, then it would be for some reason to do with this, and if he shouted now and brought the household running to his empty room, there could be nothing but more death.

His fear died in the desolation that took him for the death of Simon Peter himself, into whose face he had looked only once, and lived ever since to look again—and the desolation for all his own hopes. He could have believed, and, believing, he could have been healed. He understood now about faith. He had understood that it was not necessary for Simon Peter to come in order to defeat Simon Magus. It was not needed because his Master was already there. This he understood. Faith. It was what the Centurion had known when he knelt before Jesus of Nazareth in that town in Galilee, and begged healing for his servant. Lord, he had said, his dark head in the dust. Lord, I am not worthy that Thou shouldst enter under my roof, but only say the word and my servant shall be healed. Faith. He could have faith now, but it was too late. His mind was sick and overwhelmed with all he had lost in his one moment of lost faith on that summer night two years ago. He had not been worthy of healing or Christianity or anything. Peter had known.

"Lord," he repeated aloud into the flickering darkness. "Oh, Lord, I am not worthy." The drug was creeping over him again, and his words faded into drowsiness. With tears of misery and loss still hot upon his cheeks he fell asleep.

It was raining when he woke again, a light, steady rain that whispered on the roof above his head, and the clouded sky outside the windows was touched with the first lightening of dawn. He woke quickly, and his eyes were on the sky, instantly knowing the day and trying to judge the time. It could not be long now. He drew in his breath in a sharp cry of grief—and flung his hand up across his eyes.

For a long time he did not move again. Then, slowly, incredulously, he bent and stretched his fingers where they lay across his eyes, and felt the sweat prick out all over his body, and the wild thudding of his heart. Then he stretched his legs and bent them up beneath his chin, and waved his arms and moved his head. Quivering, he got out and stood on the floor, the soft silk of the Persian rug warm beneath his feet. Wild belief growing in him, he stepped down the two steps and walked at last across the colored floor. He paused a moment by the door, his face bemused, as if he wondered what to do. Then he lifted his eyes to the lightening sky beyond the windows.

It had been an insistence of his mother's that there should always be clothes for him. Who knew when the gods might answer all her sacrifices with healing? So in the presses in his room were tunics, sandals, togas, replaced unworn as he grew through the hopeless years. The tunic was easy. His scrabbling, unaccustomed fingers had trouble with the sandal straps; and the long folds of the toga he tossed aside in despair. It was still silent in the colonnades; the slaves were not yet awakened by the clamor of the dawn bell, and he found the small back door where Gretorix had taken him with little trouble.

He did not know his way about Rome. So many long years had passed since he had, as a little boy, gone swaying in his mother's litter through the streets. He knew he must go downward and across the Tiber, and then surely he would recognize the Vatican Hill, with Nero's Circus in the gardens at its foot. He could see it by the time he had crossed the Forum, not even glancing at the stall holders who were setting up their wares in the first gray light. The rain had stopped when he crossed the Tiber, padding over the old bridge of Agrippa with no thought any longer for the wonder of his new-found legs—only a raw, dry desperation to reach the Circus before the yellow stain that was spreading up the sky behind the Coelius should clear the last shreds of darkness and fill the city with the light of dawn.

The dead light lay only in the valleys, and the sky was streaked with scarlet behind the eastern hills, turning Tiber to a sheet of rose, when he flung himself against the high, closed gates of Nero's Circus. Frantically he pummeled on the great ornate double doors, and soon a hatch shot back and a soldier's head looked out, amazement in the stolid face under the burnished helmet.

"Get away, boy! What d'you think you're doing? The Emperor has a private party. Better be gone before you're part of it. Get on with you!"

Diomed could not speak. He could only stand, leaning on the door, dragging his breath through his dry, exhausted lungs, staring at the soldier until he shook his head and slammed the shutter closed. The great door was firm and solid once again, and the sky above the seven hills flushed bright with the pink of the advancing day. He leaned his head on the cold metal of the door and gripped his fingers round the heavy carving, trying to steady himself against despair. Suddenly he recalled his painted room long, long ago, when Demetrius had come to do his head, and there had been talk to pass the time.

"And where do you live, Demetrius?"

"I live on the fifth floor of an apartment house my young lord, beside the Vatican Hill and Nero's private Circus. The top floor. I have a free seat for the Circus if I so wish it."

Distraught as he was, he had sense not to question the few passersby who moved in the lightening streets, pausing to listen to the crescendo of shouts and cheers that rose from the red walls of their Emperor's Circus. He staggered on, counting the stories of the apartment houses. The fifth floor. The top floor. Four rows of windows. Six. The sun was coming now, clearing the last shreds of cloud and warming the morning sky to pale, brilliant blue. Now the tears lay unchecked on Diomed's face, and the shouting from the Circus rose to a frenzy of jeers and yells. One, two, three, four, five floors. The fifth was the top. He stumbled through the hall of the house at the bottom of the block and up the public stairs, up to the closed door on the fifth floor with his breath whistling in his throat and barely strength in his hands to bang upon the door.

It was Pallius who opened it at last, cautiously, and then wider to let him stagger into the room. Melas was there, and Gretorix, and Demetrius, gathered around the window with several others whom Diomed did not know. They looked at him in silence, but with no surprise, almost as if they saw something they had long expected. Only Gretorix laid a hand upon his arm as they parted and made room for him before the window.

Now it was full daylight, the bright sun of the Roman morning pouring down on the half-empty Circus and the great circle of yellow sand and the cross that was reared before the red sandstone stylus in the center. The best of the gala had been kept till last. There had been games and chariot racing and gladiator fights and a few lesser Christians executed in the blaze of flares and torches, ringing the Circus in the dark hours before the dawn. In the first sunlight, Diomed laid his hands upon the stone sill and stared down at the huge figure crucified head downward, the white hair trailing to the yellow sand that was still hazed and cloudy with the dust of chariots. He had told his judge he was not worthy to be crucified in the same way as his Master. Behind the cross the sun blazed on the gilding of the tall red stylus, and before it the sand was littered with sandals and sherbet cups and broken fruit, thrown by the jeering crowd.

"This time," whispered Diomed to himself, "he did not fail his Master."

Quietly, in the high, bare room of Demetrius, the little band of Christians knelt behind their bolted door and prayed for Simon Peter, who died for all of them even as his Master, down below them in the strengthening sun. And in a while it was all over. The bored, elegant crowds of Nero's friends began to trickle from the open gates, calling for their chairs and chattering over the morning's entertainment. Inside the arena, a dark-haired man crept from the scattering crowd to throw himself below the cross. In a moment, Mark followed him, and the soldiers watched and let them both alone.

"John," said Demetrius. "John. I did not know that he was here. The youngest," he added to himself. "The best beloved."

Pomponia came then, from where she had been with Paul, who had been beheaded as his Roman right, at the second milestone on the Via Ostia.

"The soldiers were very kind," she said. "They gave me the scarf that bound his eyes." She turned then from the window, and looked over those gathered in the room. "Remember, my children," she said, and her voice was strong and firm. "Remember what his Master said. On this Rock will I build my Church, and the gates of Hell shall not prevail against it. Nor have they, my children, today, nor will they, any other day. Because his Master said it. The dying Peter is the living Church." She passed her hand across her face and looked round again. "Now, my children, we must go. We are gathered fourteen in a room, and that is death. There is enough death today. Go carefully, a couple at a time. Go now." The first two slipped from the room and she laid a hand on Demetrius' arm.

"Demetrius, I must speak with you. There must be Christian burial for Peter and Paul."

The Greek nodded, and only then did she take notice of Diomed.

She laid a finger gently on his cheek, and the blood from the scarf of the beheaded Paul was still dark on her hands.

"Be kind, my son," was all she said. "Be kind. Go first to your mother."

Dumbly the boy nodded, unable to speak, choked in the sudden instant with the full knowledge of his healing. He followed Gretorix from the room, and they made their way down into the street, and Gretorix turned to offer his master the support of his arm.

Diomed shook his head, and in the golden sun of the early morning, he turned toward Tiber and the bridge, looking upward toward the marble masses of the Golden House, walking home himself, as in all his prayers and dreams, after seeing Simon Peter.